Under the Durian Tree

Born in Malaya in 1934, Fergus Linehan has been film critic and Arts Editor of *The Irish Times*. He has written extensively about the arts and is the author of plays, musicals and comedy material for radio and television. He lives in Dublin with his wife, the actress Rosaleen Linehan, and has a daughter, three sons and a grandson.

Under the Durian Tree is his first novel.

'The story is memorably rich. Like the jungle that inspires it'
IRISH TIMES

'In this, Fergus Linehan's first novel, he has created, in Tim O'Hagan, a character who lingers in the unconsciousness long after the book is finished'

SUNDAY TRIBUNE

'His story is poignantly engaging and enriched by just the right measure of historical and geographical detail'

BOOKS IRELAND

'The novel is a lush and compelling journey'

IN DUBLIN

'Once begun, this novel won't be put down'

CORK EXAMINER

'Fergus Linehan's first novel is a quiet and quirky piece that lingers in the mind long after it is over'

EVENING HERALD

'It is a story vivid in colour and detail, a story both of gnawing romance and of the death of love'

SUNDAY TRIBUNE

'The overall wealth of the story . . . is memorably rich, like the jungle that inspires it'

IRISH TIMES

Under the Durian Tree

Fergus Linehan

TOWN
HOUSE
DUBLIN

First published 1995 by Macmillan

This edition published 1996 by Pan Books
an imprint of Macmillan Publishers Ltd
25 Eccleston Place, London SW1W 9NF
and Basingstoke

Associated companies throughout the world

ISBN 0 330 34480 3

1 3 5 7 9 8 6 4 2

A CIP catalogue record for this book is available from
the British Library.

Phototypeset by Intype London Ltd
Printed by Mackays of Chatham PLC, Chatham, Kent

To Rosaleen, who makes
everything possible

Chapter One

THE JUNGLE. As I sit here writing I try to remember it, what made it so... compulsive. Yes, that's the word. Greenery. Trees, vines, bushes. Leaves smooth, prickly, tiny, as big as desk tops. Not much to see, though. A monkey, high above, insects, a coloured butterfly. Tigers? I never met one in forty years there.

Yet its pull is unforgettable. Its throb, the sheer quantity of it, its enveloping fecundity. Things sprout, grow, pullulate, die, decay, rot. Under the pulpy surface simple creatures, a mouth and a stomach, chew, digest, evacuate, spawn millions of microscopic eggs, larvae, wriggling pinheads. Things with legs scurry and devour things that creep, things with soft wings flutter above the ground out of which they crawled. From the rich putrefaction spring green things, shoots, vines, fruits with rank sticky juices, violent flowers, bushes and trees with great twisted trunks like elephants' legs.

Up, upwards, ever upwards, through the green twilight towards distant brightness. Up to the sun that stares down unblinkingly on the top carpet hundreds of feet above. Up crawl the plants, twisting and fighting, strangling one another, drawing the sap out of the weaker in their search for that higher world, that life-giver. And with them go the creatures, ant, beetle,

1

lizard, deer, tapir, tiger, monkey, killing and eating and impregnating until they, too, come crashing down to become part of the unending chain of death, decay and regeneration, the swarming, throbbing engine of life, life, life . . .

Life, a life. Sitting here in this cold room the mementoes seem pitifully meagre. A boar's tusk inkstand, a display of *krises*, the wavy-bladed Malay dagger, mounted on a wall. A golden picture of a Malay boy, badly painted. The obligatory carved wooden linen chest. A nest of tables in rosewood on which stand mostly chipped Chinese figurines, once a rarity but nowadays they can be bought in any oriental huckster shop in any city in Europe. Lost most of my stuff in the war. What the local looters didn't get, the British army cleaned out when they came back after it was all over. Who was it, now, that story was about? Some chap who went to the house of a colonel and found himself eating off his own dinner service. Too much of a gentleman to mention the fact.

Pictures, photographs. Who's that in the solar topi? Yes, it used to be me. Whatever about mad dogs, even Englishmen didn't go out in the midday sun without them. Look at him in the *tutup*, the white jacket buttoned up to the collar. We were expected to wear it with black shoes. There he is again with some Malay dignitaries in their ceremonial sarongs, a handsome costume. Was he really that serious, that strained?

A young woman, dressed in white, taken some time in the twenties. Serious, again. We weren't like that at all. We laughed a lot, were happy for a time, weren't we? Another of her holding a baby, my son, with his nurse, a Chinese *amah* standing beside them, calm as ever, clean as ever. And there's the boy again, aged what? Dressed in his school blazer and tie, must be about eleven. What's this he's called? Oh, of course I know. Maurice, Muiris, a good Irish name, always insisted on that. Mark of their background, even when they're far from home. With an engineering firm in Nottingham now, about as much interest in Ireland as he has in Malaya.

Is that it? Is that what I have to show for it all . . .?

Of all the fruits of the Malay peninsula the most fascinating is the durian. How can one describe its flavour, or perhaps I should say flavours? Imagine the finest strawberries, raspberries, plums and pineapples, all set in the lightest and most delicious of custards. Is it any wonder that the Malays become obsessed with it, gorging themselves on the bright yellow flesh, embedded in sections each the shape of the female womb. Endless hours are spent discussing it, examining it, shaking it to make sure of its ripeness, even sitting under its trees in the jungle waiting for it to drop, for it must never be picked. Its powers are legendary, both curative and aphrodisiac. 'When the durian falls,' so the saying goes, 'the sarong rises.'

Molly comes in to me. Everything an Irish colleen should be, down to the name: rosy cheeks; brown curly hair; dancing eyes. Straight out of one of those music hall songs – not Irish at all – which were once so popular, 'Sweet Molly-oh', 'My Darling Molly', 'Molly, My Molly, Rose of Old Mayo'.

'How are you today, sir?' says she in her rich brogue, and for all the world I expect her to curtsy, showing a glimpse of red petticoat.

'Well, I'm well,' I lie gallantly, for my chest feels tight and there's a strange pressure on my throat as if some invisible man is trying to throttle me. She looks

3

at me and I can see in the glance that I don't look well at all, not even as well as the deterioration of the years allows.

Why do we lie so much about our health? Don't want to be a trouble, don't want to be a cause of alarm, don't want to be laughed at because the whole thing is only in our imagination anyhow. Foolish old hypochondriacs, fearful of every ache and pain that moves around our ageing bodies, taking our temperatures, weighing ourselves, gazing in the mirror at the wreckage of our looks, anxiously surveying our bowel movements like priests inspecting the auguries.

Still, I don't want to put a totally unblemished complexion on things.

'It's cold,' I say.

'Cold?' says she. 'Not at all, 'tis a beautiful sunny day.'

I rub my hands together. Old man's hands, all veins and wrinkled skin. 'I'll never get used to it, I'll never get used to it.' Nor will I. We're all the same, us old Eastern hands, tempered in the tropical heat. The raw damp chill of the Irish air reaches into the marrow of our bones. We huddle over fires, wrap rugs around us, take to bed with hot-water bottles – nothing ever really dispels it.

'Was it really very hot out there?' Molly is making polite conversation. We've been through all this before, we both know, but it's kind of her. She knows I don't get much chance to talk with anybody nowadays.

'Yes,' I say. 'Yes. Some people, some Europeans could never take the heat, could never get used to it. But I loved it. I loved the heat. Hot, hot, and then all the rain. It rains, you know, nearly every day in Malaya.'

'Like Ireland.'

'No, no, not a bit like Ireland. It comes down in sheets, in buckets, nearly every day around the same time for a hour or two. And then it's gone again as quickly as it came and the sun is out, blazing, blazing, blazing . . .'

The hidden strangler has put his hands round my throat again and I suddenly feel panicky.

'Are you feeling all right, sir?' she asks.

'Oh, yes, fine, fine.' More lies. There on my desk are my notes, the shorthand of a lifetime in my spidery hand. 'Just doing a bit of work. Must keep busy.' Why must I keep busy? To make sense of it, to make sense of what happened to me. But what sense is there in a life? Or maybe it's because there's nothing else to do, nowhere else to go, no one else to talk to but Molly and milkmen and shopkeepers.

'Michael is outside,' she says.

'Michael?'

'He's come to mend the gate.'

Oh, yes, Michael, her young man. Sullen-looking Michael with the heavily brilliantined hair and the scowl on his face. I meet him on his bicycle when I'm out walking. Gives me a curt nod. Can hardly bring himself to bid me the time of day. What am I to him? I've overheard them talking in the garden outside my windows. Why does he dislike me? Tight-fisted, that's what he called me. Am I?

'Them Protestants are all the same. Tight.'

I'm a Catholic.

'Well, whatever he is, a West Briton.'

Am I? Faith of my Fathers, with an Irish brogue you could cut with a knife. Some of the ones who went out East forgot everything Irish. Remember Morphy?

5

That's the Protestant for Murphy, we used to say. Changed the accent, changed the name, changed the religion, became a Freemason and married a general's daughter. Did him no harm. Sir Thomas Morphy KCMG. What ever happened to him? Dead, I suppose, or retired to Bournemouth or Tunbridge Wells. Certainly not to Cork, where his family had a hardware business. Another old josser like me, suffering from arthritis and God knows what else, boring whoever he meets with stories of places and people they don't want to know about. Is there a place reserved for him in Irish Catholic Hell, that special corner of damnation for the sex-obsessed, guilt-wracked, priest-ridden failures of the race of the Gael? Is there a special devil to torment him for going over to the Church of England and learning to talk with the accent of Harrogate and Hastings?

With me it was different. Irish and proud of it. Never missed mass if there was a Catholic priest within twenty miles. Kept the brogue I was born with. Laid it on thicker, even.

'Begorrah, b-hoys, how are ye today?'

It probably cost me three promotions. Certainly, I was always being passed over in favour of people who hadn't half my ability, or so I thought. No knighthood for me, that meaningless accolade that means so much to so many, particularly the wives, who become Lady This and Lady That. I got a CMG after the war, what somebody called one of the consolation prizes of Empire. Good to have it, of course. It's in a box upstairs, together with its nice bright ribbon. I haven't opened it for years.

Don't misunderstand me, I'm what they call a colonialist. An Irish nationalist who believed in the British Empire, if you can square that. We believed in freedom for Ireland. Freedom, whatever that means. Our own parliament, but under the crown, as part of the Empire. Republicanism was for extremists and though our lot were viewed across the water as dangerous nationalists, we were basically conservatives, with a small c. Our own parliament with limited powers would have suited us well enough, for the time being anyway, in which Church and state would be united in preservation of the status quo. Freedom to make our own mess of things, rather than having London do it for us. Freedom for them, too, when they were ready for it. The Indians, the Malays, the Africans. Trouble was, they never seemed to be quite ready for it, or so we thought. That's why they had to fight for it, unless they were lucky, like they were in Malaya, where they got their independence by negotiation.

But a colonialist? Someone with a jackboot on the neck of a native and a rawhide whip in his hand? Draining the country of its resources, stealing the wealth that should have belonged to what were once called the lesser breeds? Malaya was a happy land, prosperous and peaceful. Its soil was fruitful and full of minerals, its people mostly contented. We held the ring between the two main races, the Malays and the Chinese, who otherwise would have been at each other's throats ... Why are we always at each other's throats? White and black, Hindu and Muslim, Catholic and Protestant, Chinese and Malay? What a species we are!

Michael. Michael stands holding his bicycle outside the back door. His trouser ends are tucked into his shoes, his suit is shiny and ageing, his face is tight at the thought of me and my hated world, a world about which he knows nothing.

Michael ... Mick. I had a brother Mick. Killed in

7

the first war. He was one of the thousands who went out from Ireland at the call of John Redmond, leader of the Irish party at Westminster who said that little Ireland should fight for little Belgium and for the rights of small nations like our own everywhere. He was in Flanders' fields with many others of his regiment, the Munster Fusiliers. They never found his body, to our knowledge. An Unknown Irish Soldier, only there could be no eternal flame, no wreaths of poppies for him in his own native land. He and his like have been written out of our history, to all intents and purposes. Backed the wrong side, their names now all but vanished, as completely as his body vanished amid the mud and bursting shells. Meanwhile those who stayed at home to fight in or support the Easter rising of 1916 against the British inherited the running of the new Irish state when it came into being some years later.

A great footballer, Mick. I think he'd have played rugby for Ireland if . . . Not big, maybe he wouldn't have been big enough. Wing forward, he could tackle like a demon, and fast too. Played for Munster, I saw him, went to Lansdowne Road in Dublin to see them against Leinster. He had a great game, scored a try, they all said he should have got an Irish trial. Next year for sure. Then the war broke out.

He'd have been, what? Nineteen? Twenty?

The durian fruit . . . stinks. The stench in your nostrils is like vomit, sweet vomit. Eating it is like eating custard in a lavatory – vile, hot, strange, sickening, sickening . . .

I am on my knees. I am on all fours. How did I get here? I can't remember falling. There's pressure, pressure, a roaring in my ears, a roaring like waves in a storm. Voices, voices coming and going. Somebody is singing loudly, discordantly. Several people are shouting together, I can't make out the words. But I'm alone, aren't I? The silent strangler has come back. I try to move. I can't. This is ridiculous. What's going on? What's it they always say in the pictures when they come round after fainting? 'Where am I?' I can see the window, the sun is shining into the room from it. Outside in the garden Molly is talking to glowering Michael. I can hear them.

'He says to go ahead with mending the gate.'

'What about the money?'

'You'll get paid.'

'Paid twopence ha'penny . . . Protestants!'

'I told you, he's not a Protestant.'

Michael is a man with few ideas in his head. But what he has he sticks to.

'Well, whatever he is,' he says yet again, 'a West Briton.'

West Briton. An inhabitant of the island of West Britain, one of the British Isles in the British Empire. A shoneen, a lickspittle, a Castle Catholic, a toady, a low fellow, on bended knee to the oppressor.

'Who says he's a West Briton?' says loyal-to-me Molly. 'He grew up here, didn't he? What else is he but Irish, you've only to hear him speak.'

I can't see Michael, but there's a sneer in his voice. 'They're the worst. Out in the British Empire, for King and country, walkin' on the faces of the local people. Ask the blacks out there what is he! Irish, me arse!'

There speaks a true patriot.

I try to call out to them but nothing comes. The room seems to be fogbound. Could it be a dream? There seems to be something of the real unreality of a nightmare. I am still on all fours, frozen in the ridiculous posture, neither up nor down. Come on, wake up. I've had dreams before in which I've told myself this isn't a dream.

Move, move, move! My body and my brain seem to be going in opposite directions. Body refuses to do what brain tells him. 'Aww! Aww! Aww!' That's coming from me, that's me trying to speak.

Wait. Yes! My hand moves, one hand only. I get hold of the edge of my desk. Shakily I pull myself up. Shakily I am standing. The room is moving, tilting crazily. I seem to be on board ship, passing through the Bay of Biscay in foul weather. I collapse into a chair . . .

Tommy Evans, aged about twenty-three, is sitting in the chair opposite, grinning. He's dressed in white, his face is brown from the sun, he's perspiring and his straw-coloured hair sits on his head like a mat.

'Hello, old boy,' he says in that Anglo-Irish accent that sounds English to the Irish and Irish to the English.

'Tommy? Tommy, is it you?'

'It's me, all right. Large as life and twice as ugly.'

'But how did you get here?'

'Spot of leave, old chap. May be making a move back here from the *ulu*.'

'That's wonderful,' I say, and so it is. He's been dead twenty years.

'They treating you all right?' he asks, and I find myself saying, 'Oh yes, very well.'

'Heard the news from home?'

Which news would that be?

'About the Rising in Dublin.'

That? Of course I've heard about that.

'Damn fools.'

'I suppose so,' I say, though I'm not so sure. Even though I doubt the justice or wisdom of it all the blood is up, the old knee-jerk anti-English thing that's part of so many Irish, made hotter by the shooting of the leaders of the rebellion.

'Even a Home Ruler must see that,' he says. 'I ask you, what's it going to achieve?'

'It's a matter of broken faith. Every time they offer us Home Rule they fail to deliver it.'

'It will come after the war.'

'Will it? Are you sure? They'll block it, they'll fudge it. The army, the Tories, the Unionists, the same old gang. They've no intention of ever letting Ireland rule itself.'

'Well, I'm just out of the jungle, so spare me Irish politics at least. Have a drink.'

'Why not? Boy!'

The Chinese boy, attentive as ever, supplies us with a couple of *stengahs*, the whiskey and water which is the staple drink of the colony, the ice already melting in the soupy Malayan heat, in the time it takes to get them from the bar. Not much whiskey compared to what you'd get at home, and plenty of water, but we make up for their weakness by the number of them we put away.

Tommy is telling me, as if it were the most normal thing in the world, about his life in the remote corner of the *ulu* or outback from which he has just returned. A steamer up the beautiful east coast (no roads in those days) to a remote harbour, three days by small boat up one of Malaya's wide brown rivers, fish eagles overhead, crocodiles in the water, eaten half-alive by mosquitoes and a God-awful din coming from the jungle every night. Then a jolting ride over rough jungle tracks in a cart drawn by buffaloes – a Malayan patriot, the buffalo, he hates the smell of Europeans.

At last the small, dusty town. The back of beyond. A couple of Sikh policemen, a Chinese *towkay* who sells everything from cooking pots to sarongs, an open-air market and the *istana* or palace of the local raja.

An old man, his brown face wrinkled like a walnut, courteous, wise, the father of his people. He's been to Kuala Lumpur, he's been to Singapore, he's even been to London, sitting among the minor nobility at some coronation or jubilee, a Nigerian chief on one side of him, an Egyptian bey on the other, behind him a West Indian baronet whose ancestors grew rich from slaves, in front of him a Polynesian princeling whose ancestors ate human flesh. He has made the *haj* to Mecca, he has seen the flash of *krises* settle dynasties, heard words of sedition against the British whispered in his ear, played both sides against the middle, backed the right one and come out a survivor. He is beloved of his people, his wives, and many of his many sons.

Now he receives an annual stipend from the British government as part of a treaty made by his overlord, the Sultan of the state, and H.M. Government, a treaty that corrals him, draws his teeth and makes over his land to the white man in all but name. It is unthinkable that he should not live in the style of an aristocrat, with palaces and a retinue and a generous hand for his many supporters. What's more, he loves to gamble, and he is always in debt. So he constantly summons to his palace, for loans, for advances, the young man, the boy, whose job it is to act as his paymaster and adviser.

Some years ago, as his faith allows, he took a new wife, though he had passed his seventieth year. She was sixteen years of age, as beautiful as a frangipani flower, as graceful as a lily, youthful enough to be the daughter of his sons. He loved her with all the foolishness of an old man besotted by a young woman. He lavished gifts on her, jewellery, richly embroidered sarongs, a motor car with a driver, though there were no roads on which to drive. He laughed uproariously at her slightest quip, made rules and laws of her whims, neglected his duties to be with her. Nobody dared say anything to his face about the impropriety, the inanity of his infatuated behaviour.

His two older wives, matrons who had long been comfortable with their positions, watched her with hatred. In the women's quarters there was much whispering, unusual visitors in the night, incantations, the mixing of potions. One morning she was found frozen in death, a flower that had been snapped off its stalk while hardly yet in full bloom.

Tommy is summoned to the *istana*. He knows, everyone knows that the other wives have had her poisoned. What to do? Reports fly back and forth along the jungle paths to the sultan, to his adviser, to Kuala Lumpur (or KL). Confidential stuff. What they contain, if it survives at all, is long ago hidden away in some dusty archive. The old man is shrivelled by grief, but he says nothing, does nothing, so nothing can be done. His ruler, the sultan, takes counsel quietly, privately. The wives are of good family. The scandal, unthinkable.

Maybe some white civil servant, incorruptible, imbued with notions of justice, objects. He is firmly put in his place by his superiors. These aristocrats are absolute rulers in their far-flung corners. Provided they make no public trouble, stir up no rebellions, they can do as they wish. If they should prove too fractious they can always be brought to heel by threatening to withdraw their allowances, in extreme conditions by exile, but that is rarely necessary. For the most part they are as honourable as, well, as English gentlemen. The sultans and their families remain.

'My old raja died,' says Tommy.

'He sounds a great character.'

'Yes, I was sad. Grand old chap, everyone loved him. He called me to his death bed: "Mr Evans," he said, "I leave you my sons. They're good boys, they have only two vices, drink and women." ' Tommy laughs.

'So now you're a step-father.'

'Deuced awkward. The youngest of them must be at least twenty years older than me if he's a day. What a funny old world. If I went home tomorrow my own father would still treat me like a child.'

We sink another couple down the hatch, and I sign a chit. We seem to be in a club, one of those clubs that are to be found the length and breadth of Malaya. This is an establishment for gentlemen and money doesn't pass hands, or not until the monthly reckoning comes in anyway. We all sign a lot of chits.

Two planters come over and join us. Not quite it. The type of fellows who marry barmaids. Campbell is large and bloated with a walrus moustache. Updike is small, weasel-faced and balding, with an accent which immediately betrays his social inferiority to his always snobbish fellow-Englishmen. Together they look like an unfunny Laurel and Hardy. Tommy does the honours.

'How do you do?'

They ignore me. Both are drunk and seem angry.

'Boy!' shouts Campbell. 'Four *stengahs*, and hurry up or I'll kick your arse.'

'Irish, eh?' says Updike, looking at me with distaste.

'Yes, another one of us,' says Tommy.

'Bloody Irish are everywhere.'

I decide to take it as a joke and smile, which is a mistake.

'Well,' asks Updike, his breath sour with whiskey and bile, 'what do you think of your damned compatriots now? Shooting British soldiers, stabbing us in the back while we're fighting the Hun.'

Campbell wakes up. 'I hate the bloody Huns,' he tells the Club. 'Met lots of 'em in Sumatra. Run a damn bad show there.'

'Surely the Dutch run Sumatra?'

It's the wrong thing to say. Anything is the wrong thing to say. Campbell and Updike exchange glances that signal, Who is this upstart newcomer anyway?

'Dutch whatever,' says Campbell, with a fine contempt for me and for everyone else who doesn't belong to the Happy Breed. 'They're all Huns to me. Bloody gin-swilling meinheers . . . Boy!' he bellows.

The Boy arrives with our drinks, not a moment too soon. 'Yes, sir.'

'About bloody time,' says Campbell.

'Yes, sir.'

'And next time I want a drink, I want it quickly. *Cepat*! Understand?'

'Yes, sir.'

The Boy puts down our drinks and retires. As he goes Campbell gives him a hefty kick in the backside.

'That's to remind you.'

'Cheers,' says Updike cheerlessly, and we return the toast.

'You know what I call those chaps in Ireland?' says Updike, always a man for the telling word. 'Traitors.'

Which, of course, should be my cue to leave. But, of course, I don't, won't, can't.

15

'That isn't how I see it,' I hear myself say.

'Don't tell me you're one of those what-do-you-call-ems? Home Rulers.'

'I believe in Home Rule for Ireland, yes.'

'Ho, ho, what have we here, Billy?' Updike asks his friend.

Campbell lowers his *stengah* and ponders. Then he finds the *mot juste*. 'A damn traitor,' he says bibulously.

Someone seems to be talking that isn't me, only it is. I'm not that sort of person, I'm not all that hot. I'm a nice, shy, rather inoffensive Irish boy.

'I'm no traitor!' I say, rather too loudly. Heads are turning from the other tables. 'Ireland has a right to govern itself. It's a separate country.'

Updike is a wit, a mimic, a master of sarcasm. 'Oh, faith and begorrah, the bogtrotters have a right to govern themselves!' He continues self-righteously, 'Ireland is part of the Empire and ought to be damn proud of it.'

Heads nod in agreement, *tuan* and *mem* nod agreement. Cheek! Who does the fella think he is? Just out from home and doesn't know his place. What are things coming to? It wouldn't have been like this in the old days. We're not getting the type of chap we used to. Irish farm boys, their heads full of God knows what mad ideas.

Even the Chinese boy, a fervent admirer of that upon which the sun never sets, silently agrees, despite the pain in his anus. Campbell seems to sense it through his drunkenness.

'Many's the poor foreign blighter would be very glad to be British, I can tell you.'

Tommy jumps into the breach. 'Steady on, chaps,' he says. 'Tim's no traitor. His brother's on active service in France.'

'Then he's a better man than his brother,' says sour Updike.

A toast. Ladies and gentlemen, charge your glasses.

Campbell is on his feet, unsteadily. 'God save the King, say I.'

Murmurs. 'The King.' Don't want to make too much of a fuss about it. Couple of drunken planters, don't know how to behave, half of 'em. Still, standards are standards. Even Tommy murmurs, 'The King.'

I've drunk the toast a hundred times, even in the short space of time I've been in Malaya. It's part of every stuffy evening in every club in every back-of-beyond out-station in the country. 'His majesty, the King', followed by 'Their Highnesses, the Rulers', meaning the Malay sultans who are nominally in charge of the various Federated Malay States.

'God save the King!' says Updike, a little too loudly in the not-quite-good-enough accent of Croydon or Ealing or wherever he comes from. He stares at me. 'Aren't you drinking?'

It's the other fellow, the fiery Irish patriot, and I haven't even been drinking heavily. Ireland boys, hooray!

'He may be your king, but he's not mine,' says the bould hayro – God Almighty! I don't even believe it myself.

Updike stiffens. Dammit, no one can say he isn't fair. 'I ask you again, the King!'

'No,' says the patriot.

Updike smiles, maliciously. 'This is a matter for the committee I'd say, Billy. We're nursing a viper in our midst.'

'Bloody fella should be sent to Coventry,' growls Campbell. 'Boy, the same again!'

The Chinese boy is there like a greyhound out of

the traps, anxious to avoid another boot in the arse, certainly, but also to show solidarity with his fellow-Britishers. For he, too, is part of that great commonwealth of man, united by love of king, fair play and cricket. Indeed he is working, working, as only the Chinese can, so that his small son can be educated on public school lines. He will send him where he will learn Latin, the works of Shakespeare and how to play badminton, in the hope that one day he will reach the highest rank that a man can attain – that of British gentleman. Perhaps the dream will come true and the boy will become a millionaire, Cambridge-educated, well-read, of impeccable taste and, eventually, one of the rulers of his country. Or maybe they will educate him to become a leading figure in the Communist Party of Malaya, suffering untold hardships in the cause of throwing the British out of the country, and maybe ending up dead in some jungle clearing, the victim of an ambush, perhaps even of the fearsome, cheerful Gurkhas, who will take his head as a souvenir.

But who's to know? Meanwhile Tommy is angry with me. 'Drink the toast. You're only making things sticky for yourself. What does it matter?'

What indeed?

Tommy was, by reason of his religion and race, unionist by inclination. But it never mattered that much to him. When the fiery nationalists with whom he went to school and university attacked him with their opinions he stepped aside, shrugged off their arguments as of little importance, made jokes. An independent Ireland, if he had stayed in it, would have meant as little to him as did the old British-ruled one. He would have played his games, gone to church, worked hard and conscientiously and been happy in either. But, in any case, it didn't arise. He had been bred for export, to be one of those thousands of young men who went out to the four corners of the globe to run the Empire, He was a good, decent, but not very imaginative man who never queried the way things were. He and I had little in common, but were friends from the time we first met as small boys, until his death.

I came, of course, of a very different creed. We were of the older breed of Irish nationalist. We deplored violence, and supported the Ireland of O'Connell and Parnell, of the old Irish Party at Westminster, constitutional means, though sometimes stiffened by an implicit threat of more extreme action. During the Land Wars, so-called, in the last century, when the tenant farmers of Ireland united to throw off their landlords, my father had a prominent role and had a presentation gold watch from his colleagues to prove it. What else would he have done? He could remember a time when his own father had had to pay his rent on his knees to the agent of a titled nonentity who spent most of his life in London.

My father had enforced boycotts, when shops had refused to serve landlords and their minions, and neighbours refused to acknowledge their existence. He had supported refusals to pay rent, tried to prevent evictions and raised money to help those who did lose their homes. He had stood by, less happily, when cattle were maimed or shots fired from behind ditches at the enemy. More than once he had been threatened with jail for his activities.

Later, though the staunchest of Catholics, he had taken the side of Parnell in the great split that rent the Irish Party at Westminster over the Chief's liaison with Mrs O'Shea, a married woman. When the local parish priest damned the lost leader from the pulpit at mass one Sunday, he had led his whole seed and breed out of the church, an event which I'm told they still talk about down there, more than half a century later. We believed in an independent Ireland, born of negotiation and still part of that wider community of nations to which history and geography tied us inextricably, not some banana republic ruled by gombeen men, which modern Ireland so often resembles.

All that went down, of course, in the rising which I was now defending. Yet the new men, the heirs of 1916, who now rule Ireland, were no different from us really. We were all the descendants of these anonymous generations of ploughboys, agricultural labourers and herders, toiling on tiny holdings which they didn't even own. We just rose a generation earlier than the new rulers, they were the sons, we the grandsons of small farmers, publicans and shopkeepers, who had clawed their way out of peasantry. Give them a generation and they'll be middle class like us.

Meanwhile, while ears are wagging, I'm repeating stubbornly to Tommy, my cheeks burning: 'It's not my king, it's not my country.'

He, too, is getting angry at my stupidity. 'Then what the hell are you doing here?' he asks.

Why was I there? Because you went out six months ahead of me from College, Tommy, and wrote home? A marvellous place, you said, an adventure, things you never dreamed of, the pay isn't half bad either and there's leave every three years. What is there at home anyway?

What indeed? I was a scholarship boy, a clever fellow. I took a first class degree in classics at College and they offered me a junior lectureship, subject to confirmation by the County Council. That was my downfall. Jobbery, venality. To get the agreement of the councillors to my appointment, money was expected to change hands. Not much, a hundred pounds would have covered the whole thing. Yes, a hundred pounds was a lot more in those days, but we could have afforded it. That wasn't the point.

The point was my father, the stern, remote pater-familias whom I feared and admired in equal proportions. To grease the hands of the petty politicians was out of the question, it wasn't our way of doing things. Let that be an end to it.

So what was there left for me at home? The third son of a family of eleven. No hope of inheriting the land, no desire to become a priest, a doctor, a teacher or an engineer. That's what they all became in time, that's what happens to the sons of strong farmers. I sat for the Colonial Service examination.

Chapter Two

'IAM directed to inform you that, subject to your being passed by the Consulting Physician to this department, it is proposed to select you for appointment to the joint Civil Service of the Straits Settlements and Federated Malay States at the rate of two hundred and ninety dollars a month. On becoming a passed Probationer, with a minimum of two years' service, your salary will be increased to three hundred and ninety dollars a month.'

Or nearly forty-five pounds. Marvellous pay in those days.

The first six in the Colonial Service exam went to India. I came seventh, consigned to the second division, Malaya.

God, I was lucky! I knew I was lucky from the first day we docked. The mystic East, the golden Chersonese. The land of spices where the dawn comes up like thunder out of China across the bay. You could smell the strangeness, even while we were still at sea. Coconut oil, cloves, pepper, foul-smelling open drains and strange-smelling people, The huge skies, the flowers, excessive in their brightness and knowing no seasons – bougainvillaea, orchids the colour of jade, jacaranda, frangipani, petrea and plumbago. Great palms, the height of a three-storey house, the flooded paddy fields, and everywhere the greenery bursting out of a red soil so rich it could produce three crops within a year. Twenty acres and you had riches there.

The sun shone with an intensity I'd never dreamed of, day after day. Then there would be, out of nowhere, a sudden gust of wind. Huge purple clouds would appear in the distance trailing curtains of rain. Lightning would crack with a frightening violence, followed by the first peals of thunder. The wind would rise, darkness would fall, the approaching storm would be like a whisper, then a swelling roar, then the first drops splattering down, then a torrent, a waterfall of rain that seemed to cover the air in a solid sheet. On and on it would go. Interspersed with ear-splitting lightning crashes and thunder like a thousand heavy guns, until gradually it lessened, passed and was gone, leaving a dripping, cooler world behind.

It was a land of wonders, of wonderful peoples. Brown graceful Malays, Chinese towkays with pigtails, dark, almost black, Tamils, big-bearded turbaned Sikhs, Japanese barbers and Siamese pirates. Hindu fakirs who stuck hooks in their flesh on feast days, and tiny aboriginal *sakai* carrying blowpipes and poisoned darts, who lived in the depths of the jungle.

And then there was us, the *tuans* in our solar topis and our white ducks, so effortless in our control, so wise, so smilingly superior. We were just. We were incorruptible, we played the game according to the rules – our own rules to be sure, but fair ones nevertheless. We were better, more competent and more dedicated rulers than those who had gone before, and I suspect those who came after us. So what lost it? Oh, I know, it was a gigantic confidence trick in so many ways. A small country half a world away holding down all those races, all those people of all those beliefs and aspirations. Sooner or later our bluff was going to be called and it would become all too apparent that we had few enough tricks in our hand.

But there was another reason, I've always thought. We were such superior people, we were so certain we were God's élite. (No one loves God's élite, maybe not even God.) We looked down on just about everyone, not just the blacks and the browns and the yellows, but all the other whites too. French, Germans, Russians, Jews, Irish – yes, Irish too. Even the loyal ones could never really be part of that charmed circle, that super race that condescended to the rest of the world.

Condescension. If the British Empire had a tomb it should have just that one word on it. That's what lost it for us. Who wants to be looked down on all the time? So the *Pax Britannica* is broken, the white man has no burden to carry any more and the sun has set on the Empire on which the sun never sets.

Paradise lost! But every paradise had its serpents, even then.

'If you marry before reaching Malaya,' went my letter of appointment, 'and if you marry during your first term of service, the government will not be liable to provide a passage for your wife, or to issue you with married quarters or with a marriage allowance.'

We met while we were both in College. I can still remember it. It was at a debate: 'This house denies that Home Rule is Rome Rule', or, 'This house agrees with Swift that whoever could make two blades of grass grow upon a spot where only one grew before, would deserve better of mankind . . . than the whole race of politicians put together', or, less pompously, 'This house denies that love is blind', something like that.

As I made my speech, full of the usual empty rhetorical flourishes that were the accepted style of public address, I became aware of her in the audience, momentarily causing me to lose my train of thought. One of the audience, a bright spark called Kelly, noticed and shouted: 'Come on, O'Hagan, stop eyeing that girl and get on with it.' I blushed hotly, as did she, and the students roared with laughter.

I was two years ahead of her. She was small, fair and the prettiest girl in her year, or so I thought. Few women went to university in those days, and they were in much demand among the male students. I plucked up courage to ask her out on the floor at a Christmas party where we met again. I remember I had a rival (damn it, what was his name?), a medical student, well got, he rowed for the college and his father was one of the first people in the town to own a car. He used to arrive on the campus in it, clad in a long coat and wearing goggles, a figure of glamour among his fellow undergraduates.

The Law Society Dance, a formal occasion, that was the big social event before we broke for the Christmas vacation. What's his name? Yes, McMahon, that was it. McMahon wanted to take her, but he missed his chance. Tommy did it. He waylaid him and started talking about cars. McMahon couldn't resist airing his knowledge, doing a bit of boasting. He was furious at being tricked, but there was nothing he could do. Meanwhile I had Eileen to myself and she agreed to be my partner.

From then on we were a pair, what they now call 'doing a line'. She was quiet and seemed gentle, though there was a steel there that you might not have noticed at first. Not really my type at all, I suppose. Oh, I know in those days women had few chances to speak out in public, they tended to stay more in the background and men made the running in all sorts of ways that now seem unjust and unfair.

But that was in public. The women of Ireland, then as now, were as humorous, quick-witted and bright as their menfolk. More so, probably. Then as now.

At that stage of my life I fell in love with any girl who smiled in my direction and many who didn't too. My ardour was only matched by my amazing powers of recovery when rebuffed. I could be head over heels about someone on Friday, heart-broken on Saturday and in love again with someone else on Sunday. There was never any question of more than a few stolen kisses; perhaps that made it all the more intense.

My only encounter of any length with a member of the opposite sex had been with Nancy, a neighbour's child. She was dark, quick-tempered, funny, full of life. She took no nonsense from me, sent me up rotten if I said anything phoney or pompous. She had a passion about her, we would have fierce rows. But she would also kiss me fiercely, and press herself hard against me, so that I would become excited. Then she would push me away with a laugh and leave me shaken and exhilarated.

We were too young. In those days men didn't marry until they were well set-up financially, so marriage wasn't even a possibility, and I don't think we ever considered it. I went to college, she stayed at home on the farm, inevitably we drifted apart.

Life can be a monster. Her father, in the manner of the times, decided to marry her off to a man much older than her, also a farmer. I suppose there were some sort of financial considerations, a dowry from her, the chance of a fat inheritance eventually from him. She fought against it in every way she could, tears, tantrums, threatening to leave home. But where could she go, what could she do? She had little education and no allies. It was a good match, wasn't it? And if she didn't do as her father ordered she could clear out, they said, they weren't going to keep her any longer.

She went to the altar white in the face, haggard-looking from crying. I was invited to the wedding. The groom was a decent enough fellow, stolid, reserved, hard-working, but almost old enough to be her father. Talk of Tommy's raja! Though in that case the ill-fated bride had been all too willing to embrace marriage with a rich old man.

Not so Nancy, sitting silent between her balding new husband and a priest at the top table of the wedding breakfast. Sitting silent through the early awkwardness, the rising hilarity as the drink started to take effect, through the speeches and the songs. Sitting silent beside him as they drove away to their honeymoon and the consummation of her unwanted marriage.

But it was not like that. It was only years later I heard what had happened. On her wedding morning there had been more storms of tears, pleas from her mother, shouts from her father. Who could not pity her, this young, beautiful girl full of life and laughter, a loveless unwanted life stretching before her? How many such were there in those days, those good old days? Finally she had agreed to go through with it, but said that she would never sleep with the man, would never share a room with him.

Well, it was better than nothing, her parents must have reasoned. Better than the scandal of the wedding guests turning up to find there was no bride. Breach of promise! Oh, my God! As to the threats of an unconsummated marriage, they would soon come to nothing as soon as the normal processes of a man and a woman living together took effect. And weren't arranged marriages very often the ones that turned out the happiest? Much more so than those so-called love matches, where the thing was in trouble as soon as the infatuation wore off.

But they had reckoned without Nancy, for from the day of her wedding until her husband's death she never entered his bed. Made no bones of it either, all her family knew, all the neighbours knew. She must have had a will of iron, for she would have been seen to be failing in her main purpose in life, to provide an heir for her husband's farm.

The family would have been called in. His and hers. Threats would have been made. Annulment, shame, disgrace. No. Priests would have been summoned, persuasive ones, domineering ones. Failing in her duty to her husband, failing in her duty to God. Sin, damnation. No. Doctors, too. Maybe 'tis medical. An examination. Nothing wrong there. Is she right in the head at all? Now, let's have a good talk, I'm sure we can solve this little problem. No. No, no, no.

I met them both, years later, on one of my leaves. They had lived together for thirty years like brother and sister. He was an old man now. I couldn't but feel sorry for him. He had done no more and no less than was the common practice, waited to inherit his land, then sought and found what he thought was a suitable wife. The fact that she was so much younger meant little, country people were not romantics. She was of good family, she was healthy, she would bear him sons. How could he, a conventional, unimaginative man, have guessed it would go so wrong? And there was no redress. He could have had an annulment, in theory, but that was unknown territory, unthinkable. So he lived on with her, quiet, hard-working, an object of pity, of mild derision behind his back, and the farm would go, in the end, to a nephew.

She too had changed. The sparkle had gone from her eyes, the corners of her mouth had turned down. All those battles, all that aridity had drained from her the humour that was her most attractive feature. Should she have conceded, let him have his child? Should she have walked away from him and taken her chance in the wide world, leaving behind home, hearth and family? Who can answer for her? I would have thought differently then, probably, but in their stubborness, their bravery, their determination not to bow down to convention I see such women now as heroines.

Meanwhile, there was Eileen. In those golden days between school and earning a living, with the buffets of life all to come, we danced, we sang silly student songs, picnicked along the river in summertime, went to parties in the comfortable middle-class houses of the town in winter, attended the opera.

It is sweet to be loved, it hasn't happened to me often. To see a face light up when you enter a room, to be sought, to speak the secret foolish language of lovers, intent only on each other. Oh, I know, there's so much rubbish associated with it. All that banality. Stupid songs, empty books, mechanical plays and films and all that cynical selling of the concept of romance. What is romance anyway? A convention invented sometime in the Middle Ages which we all subscribe to eagerly? We all have to be, at some time or other, 'in love', we must climb in and out of it as if it were a swimming pool, we must seek it and hold on to it and worship it. And yet, and yet . . . What else have we got? Without it, most of those I've met who have no intimacy in their lives seem rudderless. Include me in that. Not romance, necessarily, but love, the love of others of whatever kind.

There were walks around the town on dark evenings, coming or going to lectures, slipping away from the chaperones that those innocent times demanded, though not too rigorously. Holding hands, shy kisses under the trees, a head placed on your shoulder when you didn't expect it. There were rows, tiffs, about what? They were so trivial, someone being late, some imagined rival, jealousy, neglect at a party – they were as much for the joy of making up later as for anything else.

Was there ever any feeling at that time that anything was less than it should be? I don't think so. Maybe we were too much in love with the idea of love to look into it closely. Anyway, why should we? We were young, we were happy and it was not a period in which people poked and pried into their alleged subconscious feelings, as they so often seem to do now. Many of our friends had similar student romances, but few enough of them lasted. Tommy, I remember, had a girl, one of his own kind, the daughter of a Church of Ireland rector. She was big, fair and good at games, a capable sort of person. We used to go out cycling in groups and she was the only one would keep up with the boys. Race them up hills and, often, beat them. The other girls would lag far behind, not able to keep up or, if they were, not willing to do so, emphasizing their femininity, pretending to admire the vigour, the athleticism of the males.

For a time Tommy and his girl went everywhere together, but he became restless, felt he was being pulled into something he didn't want.

'I like Edith,' he told me, 'but that's as far as it goes. I don't want to marry her.'

'Well, then,' I said, 'you don't have to.'

'No, I don't.' I can see him scratching the back of his head in a mannerism he had. 'The devil of it is both her family and mine would like nothing better.'

'It's not they who'd have to marry her.'

'I know, I know. Damn it,' he said vehemently. 'I want to see the world, get on, get around. I want to be free to go where I want and when I want. I'll probably never marry at all.'

'The sooner you tell her, the better.'

I saw her, the night he did. Her face was blotched with tears. Tommy was a bit white about the gills, but exhilarated. He had the spring in his step of a man who had broken free. His mother, her mother, tried to patch it up, present it as a lovers' tiff, bring them together again, but he would have none of it. He could be stubborn, Tommy.

For myself I had no wish to make a similar break. I was as conventional as Tommy's Edith, who later married a curate, as suitable a match as ever he had been. For my remaining time in College I courted Eileen and sometime towards the end of that we seemed to become engaged. There was no formal proposal, I think. I remember us sitting in a tearoom and me making some remark about 'when we're married'.

'Married?' she said, blushing scarlet, as shocked as if it was a bolt from the blue, a sudden spur of the moment idea from someone she hardly knew, rather than a man who had been wooing her for two years. She didn't quite say 'this is so sudden', just, 'I'd have to think about marriage. I don't know.'

'You know I love you,' I said. 'I think we should think about it as soon as I'm qualified. The Prof has as good as told me I'll be in line for a lectureship if I get a good degree.'

She said nothing, but from the tightness with which she held my hand as we went home, and the unaccustomed passion of her kiss as we parted, for she was not an ardent girl, I knew that I had won her.

The next vacation I was invited to her parents' home. They were, well, pretty awful. Her father was a prosperous shopkeeper in a small County Limerick town, her mother a former teacher, perpetually dissatisfied with the hand of cards which life had dealt her.

They fell on me, almost with whoops of joy. I was, by their standards, a Good Match, a clever young lad with a prosperous future and, to boot, son of the well-known Mr Terence O'Hagan, owner of two fine farms of land and a former acquaintance of the great, including Mr Charles Stuart Parnell and the Reverend Father Matthew, apostle of temperance to the nineteenth-century Irish, who were much in need of it. Also a relation by marriage of his Grace the Roman Catholic Archbishop of Cork, a distant cousin on my mother's side. Short of the Prince of Wales they could hardly have asked for better.

Oh, those awful visits to her parents, those endless sessions in their parlour, specially opened for me and still smelling of must. Those interminable afternoons under the eye of a particularly revolting picture of the Sacred Heart, glaring down balefully from over the mantelpiece. The halting conversations, platitudes interspersed with aching silences. 'And how is your father? And his Grace, the bishop? A wonderful man, an inspiration to us all.' (Why, I wonder? Just by being a bishop? Neither they nor I knew much more about him.)

Tea would be served. Dark, strong tea and creamy

milk. Thick slices of bread and yellow country butter. Big brown boiled eggs. Slices of cold wet ham and tomatoes. Nasty little cakes with pink icing, so sweet they'd rot your teeth. And, beside your boiled egg: 'You'll have a drop of whiskey, Mr O'Hagan.' (In those days I hated the taste of it.) 'And sure, ha, ha, I'll force myself to join you,' pouring himself a hefty glass and ignoring the eye daggers that were flying from his wife.

He was a businessman, notorious through twenty townlands for his meanness, and the harshness with which he dealt with those to whom he had given credit. He cared for nothing but his bank balance and his whiskey and feared no human being but his wife, a formidable lady who treated him as if he was a recalcitrant member of her junior infants' class. She despised his red face, his clumsiness and lack of manners, and didn't hesitate to let him know it, but he took it all from her without a murmur. How they had ever shared a marriage bed was hard for me to imagine, but they had, in fact, three children.

There was a sister, Josie, a nun. This entailed visits to the local convent, where we were fed enormous meals of meat and potatoes, cabbage, jelly and cream, and fussed over by the sisters in their gleaming, polish-scented parlour. Josie, who had inherited some of her mother's autocratic nature, rose to be a reverend mother – the only one of the family her parents lived to see fulfil their high hopes for their offspring. She, too, ran the rule over Eileen and me and pronounced herself satisfied – the bishop connection being particularly in my favour.

There was, too, a brother, Stephen, who fulfilled the black sheep role that seems to have been such a common feature of family life in those days. I had known him, slightly, when he had been a student though he was six or seven years older than me. ('I know your son Stephen' – awkward pause. 'Ah, yes, Stephen', followed by a change of subject.) He had failed his exams for years and eventually been thrown out of College, a difficult thing to achieve in those years of 'chronic' students.

He had inherited his father's love for whiskey, to which he added his own vices of gambling and an aversion to work. But it wasn't these that brought about his downfall, it was one of the unforgivable sins of sex. His crime, a deed so heinous that it could never be spoken of, was to get one of the maidservants pregnant. This I only discovered many years later, for a curtain of silence descended on the event which not even my wife would draw for me. The unfortunate girl was packed off to a Magdalene House to expiate her sin (*her* sin!), where presumably she passed years doing the laundry of the bourgeoisie, while spending the rest of her time in equal amounts of prayer and suffering.

Stephen's sentence was transportation to the Antipodes, a one way ticket to Australia where, it was hoped, nobody from his home town would ever see or hear of him again and thus find out the nature of the horror he had wrought upon his family. The plan didn't work out altogether, though, for when he got to Liverpool he cashed in his steamship ticket and stayed on in England. What he did there I was never sure, though I gathered it was something not to be spoken of and fairly seedy. Apparently there was a wife and children, though they were never seen in Ireland as far as I know. I only met him once again, but I remember him from my first year in College. He was then what is known of as 'a gas man' – in other words, he was drunk a lot of the time.

I finished my time in university with a first class honours degree, highly satisfactory. Eileen and I travelled around, staying with friends, meeting other members of the tribe of cousins and uncles and aunts, for we both belonged to large widespread families. My father, whom we both approached in fear and trepidation, pronounced himself satisfied with the match.

I had an embarrassing meeting with her father, in which I set out my prospects and asked for his daughter's hand, for that was the accepted way of doing things then. He took it for granted I would be expecting a dowry and, despite his own and his wife's approval of me, couldn't resist trying to diddle me out of what he thought I'd expect. I've never been good about money and, as I found the whole idea of haggling over his daughter's hand distasteful anyway, I made no attempt to best him. He came away from the meeting looking delighted with himself.

'How could you?' said Eileen, her voice unaccustomedly hard with anger. 'How could you let him do that?'

'But we don't need it. We'll have enough money to live on.'

'It's humiliating. Is that all you think of me?'

She was showing a side to her that I had never really realized was there, being, in fact, her father's daughter. 'Enough' was not a word she would ever associate with money, about which she was more interested and shrewd than I could ever be. She went to her mother, who read the riot act to her despised spouse and the figures were accordingly adjusted upwards.

Then came the news of my failure to secure the College lectureship. Tommy had gone out to Malaya six months before, something he had always intended to do, for, like so many young Irishmen before and since, he could see no decent future for himself in the land of his birth. His letters home so fired me with enthusiasm that I decided that I, too, would try my luck sitting for the Colonial Service entrance examination. So, at the age of twenty-two, I secured an appointment to Malaya. For me, it was a triumph, a way out of a predicament about my future, but to Eileen and her family it was like a thunderclap. The effect on them was far greater than it was on my own family, who belonged to a less provincial, wider world, with one son already in America and another destined for the priesthood and the mission fields of China.

To the Caseys it was a disaster. How to square it with all those stories about our daughter's fiancé's job in the university, the hints of professorships to come? And it was also inexplicable. A matter of a few pounds in the right quarter, an investment, the sort of thing that Eileen's father wouldn't think about twice! Of course, they never said any such thing, being far too much in awe and fear of my formidable father, like all the rest of us. Instead the talk turned to the opportunities now opening up for young men abroad, fortunes to be made out there, wherever it was, knighthoods even . . .

For Eileen it was much worse, of course, more than the eternal fear of what the neighbours might say. I would be gone for three years, leaving her in a limbo, tied by her engagement. After that she would face married life without family or friends in a place on the other side of the world which she could hardly imagine and had hardly heard of until my decision.

Nowadays when travel is becoming universal, the

thought of going halfway round the world is almost commonplace. But in those times few people in Ireland, apart from missionaries, had ever seen an Asian or an African, let alone been to their countries. Some years later, on one of my leaves, I met a colleague and his wife, also home, who had brought a Chinese *amah* back with their small children. Crowds followed her in the street when she took their two little girls out for a walk, gawping at her as if she was something from a freak show.

Eileen was bewildered, alarmed. I should have been more understanding, I should have looked at other options, other possibilities. But there seemed so few opportunities at home and anyway I was in the grip of a new-found enthusiasm for adventure, for wider horizons, for an escape from the safe, comfortable, stuffy world of middle-class Ireland. I didn't listen to her, I didn't read the signs, I can see it now.

We spent a seaside holiday in Kerry with her family, swimming, dancing in the evenings, kissing. At night I would dream of having her lying beside me and of other, sweeter things, till I could contain myself no longer and sought solitary consolation.

Despite the fact that my head was filled with dreams of my own daring, I knew that I would miss her bitterly when I was gone. If anyone else so much as looked at her I would be consumed with jealousy, though there was little or no reason for it. A young solicitor from Tralee was always asking her to dance and once sent her flowers, which drove me into paroxysms of fury and anxiety and my friends into gales of merriment, but there seemed nothing much to it that even my over-fervid imagination could work on.

Then, returning one evening from playing golf, I

found she wasn't in the house her parents had rented for the month.

'She's gone to the dance in Ballybunion, sir,' said the maid. 'A crowd of them went over in Mr Butler's car.' Butler was my solicitor rival.

That evening I walked the beach that skirted the seaside town alone, anxiety gnawing at me, my thoughts of betrayal, of losing her, of the collapse of all my dreams of love. In my mind I saw her in the arms of Butler, laughing, looking up at him with love, telling him things that she once told me, as the song says. It was all rot, of course. A bunch of young people had decided on the spur of the moment to go over to the dance and Butler had provided the car, no more. But why had she not told me? Why hadn't she left some word? At first she seemed amazed, then there was the inevitable row, but more furious than it had ever been. The engagement was off, we weren't speaking to each other.

Next day I packed my bags and went home. A week passed, no word at all from her. Maybe she was relieved, maybe she saw it as a way out for herself. I was the one who caved in, of course. Went to her house, apologized for my stupid behaviour, begged her to forgive me.

I can see her face. She is looking at me with that sudden shrewdness you could very occasionally notice. Not hard but level-headed, weighing things up, different from her usual gentle, smiling look. What was she thinking, what was she calculating, what were her real feelings? Then she kissed me gently on the cheek, my arms were around her and all was well again. I know now that, in those few moments, it could as easily have been all over between us. How deeply did she ever care for me, I sometimes wonder. If there's always a lover and a loved I was undoubtedly the lover. In different circumstances, would things have worked out all right between us, or was what happened in some way inevitable?

Chapter Three

I AM sitting at a shaky table whose legs rest in bowls of paraffin to stop the ants from climbing them. The ferocious insect life of the Malay peninsula is hurling itself against the mosquito nets in an effort to incinerate itself in a sexual ecstasy on my oil lamp. A beetle the size of a match box flies full pelt into the wall, flops onto the table and crawls around. There are grasshoppers and moths, green, brown, black and red-striped, and tiny ones that are triangles of delicate pearl. Winged ants and long-legged flies patrol the night, mosquitoes whine like dive bombers and wait to bite. Fearsome-looking spiders the size of a fist (harmless I'm told) scuttle along the floor. The little insect-eating lizards, which the Malays call *cicak* from the sound they make, range the walls, defying gravity while they feast on the abundance available. Now and then you see them staggering from a particularly large moth, whose wings protrude from their mouths. When frightened they have a habit of dropping their tails, which remain wriggling after their owners have left them.

I am writing home.

My darling:
I miss you more than I can say. It can be lonely here, but this country is wonderful and

*I look forward to the day when I can show it
to you. Two years 'til I get my first leave and
can hold you in my arms again. It seems for
ever! Last week I had an adventure . . .*

The girl must have been about twelve years of age.
She was engaged in some task in a jungle clearing,
cutting or planting, I don't know. Somehow she disturbed the wild boar, maybe got too near the sow and
the piglets, 'bonamhs' as we call them in Ireland. Whatever the reason, he attacked, and at a speed that gave
her no chance to escape. Those wicked, scimitar tusks
found her side and when he was done she had been
ripped open from thigh to armpit.

She lay in an *attap* hut on stilts, white and still,
when I was called. There was no doctor within reach,
so I had brought a first-aid kit and cleaned her up as
best I could. But it was clear to me that she wouldn't
last until morning. The Malays called in a *bomoh* or
medicine man, and as I could do nothing for her I was
in no position to complain. He arrived, a wizened old
man in a sarong, who spat copiously and laid a number
of leaf packets on the ground which contained various
unidentified powders. I decided to leave him to it.

But the problem of the boar still remained. Obviously, I was expected to do something; the fact that the
creature was in no way to blame for what had happened and would probably never attack another human
was neither here nor there. In the eyes of the people
he was a killer and, as I represented the law, I was the
one who would have to execute him. I had a gun, but
little practice in using it. I'd taken pot-shots at birds
and, once, on a trip into the *ulu* with Tommy, I'd
bagged a mouse deer, a little creature that lay there

with its flanks heaving after my shot had brought it down. Tommy had finished it off, but for me that was the end of my hunting career. Call me a sentimentalist, but I don't enjoy inflicting pain or death on anything.

Like it or no, though, I was going to have to do something about the wild boar. Gun under my arm, I allowed myself to be brought to the location of the attack, hoping secretly that by now the boar and all his family were miles away. We spent a couple of hours nosing round, with the help of the local villagers, but were getting nowhere and were in fact just about to go home when something moved in an area of long grasses.

It must have all happened very fast, though in retrospect I see it as one of those slow-motion things they do in the cinema now. The Malays scattered, making for the surrounding trees, and I was left on my own. Suddenly the boar burst out of the grass and charged. He was an ugly fellow, big as a calf and built like a tank, and he came at me like an express train. If I'd had time to think about it I'd probably have bolted, too, but there was nothing I could do but raise the rifle to my shoulder and fire. Nothing brave, nothing heroic, I had no other choice. Of course, when I told the story afterwards I played down that aspect of it.

I can't even say I took aim, but my shot hit him on the shoulder and knocked him down. He half raised himself on his haunches, but by now he was near enough and I had time enough to put a second bullet through his head.

I suppose it's the closest I ever came to being one of those heroes of the Empire they used to write about in *Chums* and the *Boys Own Paper*.

Bob Lionheart stood in the clearing while the

ugly beast lay dead at his feet. The natives, rushing from the safety of their hiding places, clustered round cheering and patting him on the back. The terror of the *kampung* would terrorize no more . . .

Being pork, there was nothing the Malays could do with the meat of the boar, which was pretty tough anyway, for he was an old fellow. But I hacked out his tusks, and had them mounted rather handsomely on a teak base decorated with silver, and sent home to Eileen.

The girl, I'm glad to say, contrary to my expectations, not only survived but thrived on whatever mixture of herbs, mud and incantations the medicine man administered. It's a profession that still thrives out there, with Chinese and Thai *bomohs* as well as Malays and both men and women practitioners. What's more, their cures often seem to work, on the basis, I suppose, that the best medicine you can have is a visit from the doctor. Though there's no problem for the Indians and Chinese, whose religions are flexible in their tenets, the magic practised by these people seems to have little to do with the beliefs of Islam and probably pre-dates the arrival of the major organized faiths into the area. Still the Malays are as fervent believers in this good magic as anyone else, covering the contradictions with a certain amount of mumbling of Islamic prayers by the *bomoh* while he is at work.

My triumph, of which I at once wrote to Eileen, did not bring the admiring response I expected.

Your letter arrived today. It was wonderful to hear from you, but I am very worried. Your Malaya sounds so . . . [I can see her searching for the words] . . . strange.

No, no, you'll love it. I'm falling in love with it more and more, so you must love it too. I love the rhythms of it all. The quiet life of the *kampungs*, the fishermen in their graceful boats, the spectacular sunsets, the smell of spices as the women prepare the evening meal, the men at play spinning tops and flying kites, the village gathered to watch the Javanese shadow plays, performed by a travelling showman with leather puppets. I love, too, the cleverness, the adaptability of the Chinese, the earnest Indians with their slightly comical English, the tiny wild aboriginal people who vanish like wraiths into the mysterious jungle.

Never. I'll never see it again. Never is a word like a stone in my heart.

'Surely it's not your work,' writes Eileen, 'to shoot wild animals? Shouldn't that be left to a policeman?'

I am the policeman here, and the judge and jury, and even sometimes the defence.

'Be sure not to go out without your hat, and be careful what you eat ... It seems such a wild and dangerous place.'

No, no it's not.

'I miss you so much. Do you remember that evening we sang at the piano in the parlour?'

> I'm sitting on the stile, Mary,
> Where we sat side by side,
> On a bright May morning long ago,
> When first you were my bride,
> The ... the ...

I'll try again: 'I'msittingonthestileMarywherewesatsidebyside, onabrightMaymorningwhenfirstyouweremybride ... when first you were my bride.'

How does the bloody thing go? Damn it, I've sung it so often that I get bored with the sound of my own voice when I get up at parties.

'I'm sitting on the stile, Mary . . . I'm si—' The words sound like a meaningless gargle in my throat.

Molly has come back into the room and is looking at me, white-faced.

'What's the matter, sir? Are you all right?'

'Fine, nothing to worry about. Just a little faintness, better get the doctor, though,' I say, only I can't say it. More gargling. 'Waaah, waaah, waaah—'

'What?'

'Waaa—'

'Is it paining you?'

I manage to shake my head.

'Michael's gone to the village to get some nails. Look, don't move out of that chair, sit still. I'll ring the doctor.'

'Waaah, waaah.' What's happening?

She remembers. 'Oh, no, the phone's not working, is it?'

Got it disconnected. What was the point? Who ever rang me? Maurice, once or twice a year. A wrong number was an event. What was the point of having it?

'Look,' says worried Molly, 'I'll run after Michael. He can go for the doctor on his bike.'

'Waaah.'

'Just stay there. Just stay still, Mr O'Hagan, and you'll be fine. Would you like a cup of tea?'

'Waaah.' (Yes, I would.) She takes it as no.

'Right, I won't be long. Stay quiet.' And she's gone.

I am alone. God, but it's cold! Shakily, one step in front of the other, I go to my desk and lower myself into the chair. My notes are scattered around, my memoirs. What do they mean? Why do I bother? *An Irishman in Malaya*, *Eastern Horizons*, *Wildlife of the Federated Malay States*. I've seen so many of them, so many unreadable and unread books.

I had been sent to Coventry. It was a sensation in the Club at the time, but it really didn't take very much to make a sensation in that backwater. The committee had met to consider my misdemeanour. There were those who maintained I should be expelled altogether, cast into the exterior darkness for my insult to the king-emperor. Others argued that an apology would be enough, and Coventry was decided upon as a middle way until such time as I had expiated my sin. You may think it a mild enough sentence, given the gravity of what I had done. (Yes, gravity. I was an employee of the Crown, after all. What, I wonder, would happen to an Englishman who refused to drink the toast of Ireland in an Irish club? A punch on the jaw, probably.) But to be sent to Coventry was to be cut off from all available social contact in a place which could be lonely enough anyhow. Tommy had gone up-country again and I was alone.

In my foolishness and stubbornness, instead of staying away, I went to the Club about a week later, where I had the misfortune to meet Mrs Gordon, wife of a doctor and queen bee of the local memsahibs. When I entered she and her coterie were playing bridge, a favourite pastime of white women in the East.

'Well!' she said loudly, drawing herself up to her formidable almost-six feet. 'Well! Is there no limit to the brazenness one has to suffer these days?'

Mrs Laing, her first lieutenant, an over-thin, bird-like woman, giggled loudly, her stock reaction to nearly everything.

'I fail to see what's funny about it, Mrs Laing,' said Mrs Gordon. (Though they had known each other for years the ladies still called each other Mrs This and Mrs That.) 'If certain people cannot behave themselves in the most elementary manner, one would think that they would at least have the, the . . .' She searched for the word.

'Hee, hee, the perspicacity,' said Mrs Laing.

'The elementary good manners,' said Mrs Gordon, 'not to go where they are not wanted. But then we're not getting the kind of people out here that we used to . . . not at all. Your lead, partner,' she said, and they continued with their cards.

My cheeks burning, I found myself a place at the other end of the room. The inhabitants of the tables on either side of me got up and walked away.

'Boy!' I called. There was a long wait. Finally he came, his face impassive.

'A *stengah*.' His eyes flickered sidewise for a second, trying to find out if he should serve this bounder, this cad who would dishonour the flag. Someone must have nodded, for off he went without a word. I waited, interminably, while conversation in the Club seemed to come to a halt. Eventually my *stenga* arrived, I gulped it down and left. Behind me, as I went, I could hear the sound of talk rising again, and of laughter.

During the day I did my work, in the evenings I sat alone in my bungalow. One night, driven by loneliness, I went to the town and into a bar. A crowd of Chinese were sitting round a table playing mah-jong, shuffling the ivory pieces and chattering volubly. When they saw me they grinned widely, but I ignored them and again sat alone, ordering myself a beer.

An earnest Indian taxi driver, whom I knew slightly,

came over to me. Obviously, word had got around about me.

'Bloody good,' he said to me. 'Bloody damn good.'

'I beg your pardon?'

'I am a great admirer of your Irish revolution,' he said. 'The oppressed peoples of the world must unite to entirely expel the British. See here.' He pulled from his pocket a tattered scrap of paper. 'I have been making a list of the greatest men who have ever been living.'

I nodded wordlessly.

'The Buddha, Jesus Christ, Mr Gandhi.' He beamed: 'And to these I have been adding the late Mr Patrick Pearse who fought so bravely for the freedom of your country.'

I thought of explaining that, while I was in favour of a measure of Irish independence I actually had reservations about what had been happening in Dublin, but it all seemed so complicated, so difficult to explain and so far away, that I felt dispirited.

'Thank you,' I said, meaninglessly, and left.

'Maybe we could be having meetings to discuss matters of social and political natures,' he called after me as I went. I didn't look back.

Next day I had a call to my bungalow from one of the mah-jong players, a Chinese *towkay* whose rapaciousness reminded me of nothing so much as my father-in-law-to-be, back in Ireland. With him he brought a large hamper containing bottles of brandy and champagne, tinned hams, an untimely Christmas cake, also tinned, and all sorts of other food and drink. He suggested to me, subtly, that if I would use what he seemed to think was my considerable influence to secure certain contracts for him, there would be more where that came from, as well as a hefty sum of cash.

I'm afraid I lost my temper completely. I roared at him, cuffed him, threw the hamper at him and chased him down the driveway, shouting and swearing.

Not everyone among the white community was unkind to me. Some of them ignored the Coventry business, in private at least, and after a week or two Chambers, a fellow civil servant and one of the senior men in the Club came to me and suggested that a letter of apology to the committee would meet a favourable response. By then I was only too glad to comply.

Deeply regretted my action. Too much to drink, had not intended insult. Unforgivable, but hoped they'd forgive. Yours in abasement, etc . . .

And that was the end of it, more or less. An unfortunate affair, most of them would have thought, but young chaps are apt to misbehave when they've had a few too many. Most of them had forgotten what the row was all about in the first place, if they'd ever known. Apart from the Irish out there, the politics of Home Rule were, quite rightly, a matter of complete indifference to most people.

Mrs Gordon, it is true, always treated me thereafter with the disdain a lady of the manor might show to some upstart peasant, but then that was her attitude to most people anyway. The incident lived on, too, in the way such things do. Years later, I was introduced to a major in the army.

'Oh, yes,' he said, 'you're the one got into trouble about the loyal toast, aren't you?'

I admitted as much.

He roared with laughter. 'Jolly good! There's far too much of that sort of stuffiness out here, don't you think?'

Inevitably, I was soon moved again, to a new area

of rubber estates. The glamour of the East, the planter's life! The British had stolen the rubber tree and smuggled it out of Brazil, where it was indigenous. They had brought it to Malaya and, before you could say all's fair in love and business, they'd cornered the world market. Fortunes were made – and lost when prices slumped – as my new homeland supplied the material that made the car tyres and the contraceptives of the world.

The rubber plantation is not one of the greatest scenic attractions, as I discovered when I received an invitation from Campbell to visit – yes, the same Campbell who had been responsible for getting me ostracized in my last posting. You may wonder why he would want to have anything further to do with me, but the truth was that he had long forgotten my short-comings as an imperialist, if he had ever really been aware of them through the whiskey mists that so often closed in around him.

Meeting me one evening in the Club, which inevitably provided the social centre of my new area, he had greeted me like a long-lost brother and insisted I spend a night at the large estate to which he, too, had been moved and which he now managed for one of the British companies which ran them all over Malaya. As I arrived the night was starting to fall, suddenly, as it does in the tropics. By the last light a number of flying foxes passed overhead, huge bats, almost as big as vultures, their leathery wings making a rhythmic beating sound as they went by. Apart from their passing a great silence pervaded the air.

Campbell greeted me, drink in hand, and immediately bawled for another one for me. A tiny and beautiful Siamese girl, who looked about fourteen years of age, handed it to me silently, bowed and vanished.

'Pretty bloody good, eh?' said Campbell, indicating his domain with a wave of the hand.

'How big is it?' I asked him.

'About five miles in every direction.'

I pretended to be impressed.

'Ten miles in every direction,' he said.

'I thought you said—'

'Or maybe it's a hundred and ten – what bloody difference does it make? Look at 'em.'

Truth to tell, it was a dispiriting sight. When you've seen one rubber tree you've seen every rubber tree God ever made. As vegetation goes it is an unimpressive specimen. The trees stretched, evenly spaced, in unbroken straight lines for as far as you could see, coming almost right up to all four sides of the bungalow.

'Pretty damn depressing, eh?' said Campbell moodily.

I tried to protest. 'Well, I suppose—'

'Depressing, damn depressing, can be. Sitting here, not a sound except the crack, crack, crack of the nuts on the trees as they split and fall. Month after month, year after year. It can get to you, old boy, if you let it.'

It was so obviously true that there seemed no answer.

'Hear about young McDonald in the next plantation?'

'Shot himself, didn't he?'

'Cut his throat. When they went to collect his body they found six months of letters from home, unopened.'

'Good God!'

I thought of McDonald, a pasty-faced young Scot I'd met a couple of times briefly. I thought of him sitting there in the silence, night after night, alone. The letters, from mother or sweetheart or friends, laboured over, posted, crossing half the world and lying there, untouched. What family dramas did they contain, what hopes, what fears, what disappointments? The knife, the blood . . . there must have been a lot of blood.

Campbell must have noticed my face. 'Mustn't let it get you down, mustn't let it get you down,' he said with a ferocious joviality which managed to be utterly cheerless. 'Ah, Sing!' he bellowed and a Chinese girl emerged from the rear of the house. He spoke to her in Malay.

'Just telling her you'll be staying the night,' he said to me.

'Yes, I'm beginning to get the hang of the language.'

'Needed a woman,' he said, returning to the subject of the unfortunate McDonald.

'A wife,' said innocent me. 'I suppose so.'

'Not a wife necessarily, a woman. Damn fool fell for the wife of the D.O.'

Yes, I had heard, we had all heard. What was she like? Pretty, plain, young, old, kind, harsh? It hardly mattered. In that remote largely male society we all fell, to a greater or lesser extent, for the few European women who were around. The paleness of their skin, their speech, their dress made them unattainable objects of our desires, desires which most of us never dared mention.

McDonald, though, had let his feelings show, had mooned around after the D.O.'s wife like a lovesick calf, or so they said in the Club. (It had all happened shortly before my new posting.) They had played tennis and bridge, he had chauffered her around the area. Did anything of a sexual nature take place between them? I doubt it, for if even the briefest of kisses had been discovered, it would have been magnified by the Club into full-scale passion, and the lady's reputation was still unblemished.

What did he dream of in his rubber-surrounded hell? The consummation of all his secret and not-so-secret passions? Embraces, kisses, tongues, inter-acting bodies, sexual ecstasy through the hot nights? An elopement? Driving away secretly to Singapore, then back home and happy ever after?

Of course it was never on. Her husband, like all District Officers, was moved on to a new posting and she went with him. Who knows what regrets she had at parting from her admirer? We are all flattered to have someone fall for us, it's difficult to be too hard on a person who's head-over-heels about us. But there comes a point at which all but the most foolish, the most muddle-headed, the most romantic, the most infatuated (call them what you will) pull back. Did she ever consider throwing up her marriage, everything, for this young man? Was she heartbroken, indifferent, unaware, or was it all just a joke to her? Just another of the many things I'll never know.

Whatever she thought, it finished McDonald. For a year he sat there, going out by day to do the tasks of a planter, returning at night to survey the endlessly straight lines of trees leading nowhere. Out in the back in the servants' quarters a noisy, vibrant life went on. Children were born, grandparents died, quarrels took place, money changed hands, marriages were arranged, the inter-racial brew sizzled and stank. Mohammad, the Malay *sais*, or chauffeur, detested Lee, the Number One Boy, a Hainanese Chinese who loathed Cookie, a Cantonese, and they were all joined in despising Chandran, the Tamil gardener.

But in the bungalow McDonald sat alone, nursing

his whiskey and his broken heart. No future presented itself to him but latex and malaria. No one bothered to console him or talk to him about his troubles and, for his part, he was either too shy or too bitter to confide in anyone. He sat there until the night he took his razor and, with one swift stroke, took his head half away. Messy. Very. Poor devil.

'I said to him,' said Campbell, 'get yourself a sleeping dictionary.'

'Sleeping dictionaries' was the term for non-European women kept by some planters to console themselves for the loneliness and boredom of their existence. They could be Chinese, Indian or Siamese, but hardly ever Malay – that race mixed puritanism and hypocrisy to a degree that could only remind me of Ireland. Indeed, if you so much as tried it you were liable to get thrown out of the state by the Sultan or his minions.

'Roger away to your heart's content *and* learn a language,' explained Campbell. 'By the way, which of my daughters would you fancy?'

His 'daughters', of whom there were heaven knows how many others besides the two I had met, was the term he gave to his harem out at the back. Though they had become quite famous, and the occasion of much sniffing among the *mems*, they were not usually seen around when Europeans came visiting, so I suppose I could consider myself honoured in a backward sort of way.

Well, I was shy, I came from a very different sort of world, and I was in love and engaged to be married. I made some sort of mumbled excuse about being tired, and that, I thought, was that.

'Nice girls, my daughters,' was all Campbell said,

and called for more whiskey. Unlike the majority of my fellow-countrymen it was a drink which I had never really fancied before going to Malaya. The taste I found obnoxious and the aftermath highly unpleasant. But in the heavy-drinking world of the colonies I quickly developed a liking for it and learned to put away the stuff in quantities that still amaze me, and with surprisingly little ill-effect. I can't do it any more, of course. A couple now and I'm three sheets in the wind, which may be all to the good. In fact, without whiskey my retirement would be even more bloody awful than it is.

Like it or not, we both started on our evening's *stengahs*, Campbell and I. By God, we did drink a lot in those days. Then, as now, it helped to make life bearable. It was cheap, three Straits dollars or about seven shillings and sixpence for a bottle of whiskey, half that for one of gin. And so we drank into the night, convincing ourselves that we were in the most interesting jobs in the most interesting of places, that yes, we had done the right thing in leaving home, telling each other the jokes and anecdotes which we had heard a dozen times before, sprinkling our conversation with Malay words, *makan, gaji, barang, baju*. I can't help thinking sometimes, in my bleaker moments, that it was a second-rate, second-hand existence.

It was early to bed and early to rise in the rubber plantations, as I was to discover, and I can't remember what time it was when we hit the hay. What I do remember, though, was waking up in the darkness with a dry mouth and a throbbing head, reaching over for the light and finding a small brown body beside me. A hand came across and expertly massaged my member, which sprang to attention with all the fervour of an Irish Volunteer, thinking of the day when the land he loved would be free from the tyrant's yoke.

I was a well-reared boy from a good Catholic background. Fornication was a sin, the greatest of all sins probably, and though I was not so innocent as to believe it never happened in Ireland it was, to say the least, uncommon in the circles in which I moved. What's more I was M.C.S., Malayan Civil Service, the *crème de la crème*, what they called 'the heaven-born', though that title was not, I think, meant to be complimentary.

We were supposed to show an example, keep up standards. We ranked in the social pecking order above the doctors, the police and customs men, let alone the remittance men, the black sheep and the other riff-raff who were to be found among the planters. There was no question of us visiting the brothels of Singapore or KL as other white men did, and any lasting relationship with a non-European woman would probably have resulted in a sacking.

But I was in my twenties, thirty miles from the nearest town and alone in the tropical night, so what followed followed. I'm sure I was clumsy and inept, but what of it? My partner of the night made up for my inexperience and it was better than I could do now, anyway.

I thought later of confessing all to Eileen, but of course I never did. What would have been the point of it? Oh, I know, complete honesty with each other and so forth. But it would have shocked her and hurt her and she would have found it almost impossible to forgive, so I never said anything. I did confess it to a priest – in those days I still went to confession, much as I hated it. One of those remote, very foreign, foreign missionaries from France, who by some quirk of history served in the British colonies of the Malay peninsula.

Good heroic men, who seemed to me harder to get to know than any of the Asians. Men who toiled through lifetimes among their small Chinese and Indian flocks, never making so much as a single convert among the Malays. I can't remember the occasion. What would have been the reaction to me and my fall? Three Hail Marys probably, small potatoes compared to the shock, the horror, the threats of eternal damnation that would have greeted me had I sought shriving for a similar offence back home.

Anyway, I had little time for either remorse or a repeat performance, for I had hardly seemed to have fallen asleep again when I was awakened by the blast of a trumpet. I lit a match with a shaky hand and looked at my watch. It was four o'clock in the morning.

Campbell appeared at my door. 'Time for muster,' he said, ignoring my bed-mate.

Shakily I got up and dressed. Campbell was waiting with a car. We drove through the darkness, the headlights lighting up the greenery and the white trunks of the rubber trees. Behind it everything was a dark mass, lit only by the pin-prick lights of fire-flies which seemed to make the blackness even more intense. In the distant jungle a troop of monkeys howled. For once it was blessedly cool.

Then, in the beam, a procession of ghostly white-shrouded figures appeared, shuffling along by the light of smoky firebrands, each carrying a bucket which clattered and clanked in the morning silence. It was the gang of Tamils who worked as tappers on the plantation, drawing the sticky liquid from the bark of the trees. As they went their headman swore and cursed at them, men, women and children, and apparently threatened them with extreme violence.

'All for our benefit,' said Campbell. 'If we weren't here he wouldn't be saying anything.'

The headman raved on, drawing attention to the fact that the men were all cuckolds, the women prostitutes and the children their illegitimate offspring. He waved his arms at them, his eyes bulging with rage, the muscles on his neck swelling.

We had arrived at the *padang*, an area of flat ground, and the tappers lined up in two columns. A Tamil clerk, dressed in khaki slacks, stepped forward and by the light of the lantern started to read an interminable list of names, each being answered by a grunt to denote 'present'. Meanwhile Campbell and I marched along the lines like dignitaries taking the salute from a guard of honour.

Occasionally there would be a burst of giggles or a row about the ownership of a bucket or a chisel for cutting the bark of the trees, but a look from Campbell would restore order. Next came the roll call of the children's gang, boys and girls between ten and twelve, then the weeders who fought an unending battle to keep the jungle from reclaiming the plantation, and the factory workers who processed the latex which came from the trees into big flat rubbery sheets for transportation all over the world.

There they all stood, occasionally pleading a strain or a sickness which required the attention of the dresser, whose main task, however, was to spot malingerers. The morning air, the rows of black faces, and Campbell striding up and down keeping an eye on it all reminded me in some funny way of home, of my father and brothers inspecting our cattle. I wondered, were these people any worse off than Jamesy or Mikey or the other ragged farm labourers of my youth? They too lived in homes that were little more than shacks, they too had a patch of ground of their own in which they grew some vegetables to supplement their meagre wages, they too seemed to ask for little more, or so we thought in those days, though now, I'm sure, that was not true.

Muster over, the Tamils split into gangs, each under its own self-important leader, each working a specific area of the plantation. There they would cut the bark of the rubber trees in a thin spiral, so that the sticky fluid dripped into little cups attached to the trunks. When this had hardened they put it into bags they carried round their shoulders and eventually it was brought back to the factory. The weeders pulled up every plant they could find around the trees, watched out for rotten or diseased branches, cut out cankered wood, or disposed of the many trees blown down by the short-lived but violent Malayan storms.

For Campbell and I it was back to the bungalow and breakfast in the rapidly rising heat. It was not a meal for the faint-stomached. None of your light repasts, none of your tropical fruits here, either. This was a full English breakfast, porridge, great mounds of bacon and eggs, sausages and fried bread, tea, toast and marmalade, for all the world as if we were at home on a cold winter's day.

The *tuans* may have been far from home but they tried to make as little of the fact as they could. In a land which abounds in wonderful food they still ate brown windsor soup, lamb chops and boiled potatoes (though these often had to come out of a tin), followed by spotted dog or treacle pudding. When I first went out many of them still dressed for dinner, and it was regarded as 'bad form' in many places not to don black trousers, a white mess jacket and a shirt with a stiff collar which would quickly go limp in the heat, even in some back-of-beyond jungle clearing, for all the world like figures from a *Punch* cartoon.

Probably on account of this monster breakfast, nature called, and I asked Campbell to direct me to his lavatory. His 'thunderbox', he told me with obvious pride, had been designed by himself. Clutching a supply of lavatory paper and a month-old copy of *The Times* for reading, I headed to a nearby clearing in the endless rubber forest, mercifully well out of sight of strangers. To my surprise I found myself confronted with a two-seater, one beside the other, but thought no more of it and settled myself down.

My peace wasn't to last long, though, for to my intense embarrassment I was joined by Campbell, who lowered his trousers and sat down beside me, chatting away and even peering over my shoulder to check the cricket scores in the newspaper which I'd been reading.

This uneasy arrangement was interrupted by a honking, whistling sound. A huge, ungainly bird was passing overhead, the awkward flapping of its wings produced a sound like creaking bellows. It was a hornbill, a big black and white specimen with a huge proboscis – a rare enough sight, even then.

But I didn't get long to admire it. An unmerciful explosion beside me made me leap into the air.

'Damn,' said Campbell, a large revolver still smoking in his hand. 'Damn, I missed him.' He looked over at me. 'I say,' he said aggrievedly, 'you've completely ruined *The Times*!'

Chapter Four

FOR TWO years I laboured from end to end of Malaya – they moved us around a lot in those days. The country was being turned from a feudal society into something approaching a modern state and, in my junior way, I helped with the setting up of schools, the building of roads where once there had been jungle, the establishment of hospitals, the laying down of laws and the million-and-one rules and regulations of the world today. Then I was sent back to KL, where by good fortune Tommy was also posted, the first time we had been in the same area together.

We shared a house with another young MCS recruit and lived a congenial bachelor life. We had, of course, servants and plenty of free time from our work. Sport was the centre of our lives, swimming, tennis, even rugby, though the climate was really too hot for it. Many of those out there, in the police or the commercial fields particularly, owed their appointments as much to their prowess on the playing field as to any intellectual accomplishments, indeed my own success in getting my job was probably helped by the fact that I was a relatively useful wing three-quarter. There were cups and competitions, but it was considered bad form to take them seriously, or anyway to show it. Particularly looked down on was training, which didn't mean getting fit or practising – no one did that, even the most keen – but cutting down on one's drinking or on late nights when a match was coming up.

Truth to tell, we probably all drank far too much, but we were young and, in the climate, it didn't seem to have as much effect as it would have had at home. At the end of the working day, the three of us would cool off by ladling water over ourselves from a man-sized stone jar that was kept in the bathroom, then change into sarongs and sit out on our verandah drinking *pahits*, gin or cocktails, before dinner some-where. This would involve further drinking, and then one would get down to the real business of the evening, *stengahs* until it was time to turn in.

One evening Tommy told me that he'd been asked to dinner at the house of a colonel, an Irishman who was commanding a British army regiment that had recently been stationed in Malaya, and that he'd wangled an invitation for me, too.

I remember I felt tired and didn't want to go, prob-ably as a result of too heavy a night the night before.

'You've got to come,' said Tommy. 'I want you to meet somebody.'

'Who?'

'You'll see when you get there.'

'Aha! And who is this mystery girl?'

'How do you know it's a girl?'

'Of course it's a girl. Who is she?'

'You'll see.'

Like the rest of us Tommy had had his crushes on various girls, but they had come to nothing. The number of eligible women was so small, the competi-tion so keen and the likelihood of being transferred to another part of the country so great that it always seemed a minor miracle when a romance blossomed and bloomed into marriage out there.

There had been a mild flirtation, if that's the word, with the nice, plain daughter of a missionary – he seemed to have a penchant for the offspring of the clergy. He had taken her and her mother driving a lot, attended what seemed to me an inordinate amount of services and church-related functions, and even helped to conduct Sunday School. But, inevitably, he'd been moved on and it came to nothing.

We dressed for dinner and my *sais*, Kassim, drove us to Colonel McKenna's place, one of those big handsome colonial houses, surrounded by verandahs to mask the direct glare of the sun and designed to catch every cooling breeze and draught. He and his wife greeted us. They were both in their fifties, he of military bearing, she a handsome woman with grey hair. I felt at home with them instantly.

They were of a type more common than you might think, Irish and Catholic and proud to be both, nationalist by sympathy despite the war that had made them seem enemies to so many of their fellow-countrymen. They kept a house in Mayo, where they went when he was on leave and to which they planned to retire. He had joined the army, like so many Irish, because his own country seemed to have little to offer him. He had fought against the Boers and then, with distinction, in the Great War, in which he had been wounded, twice decorated and, as so many of his fellow-officers fell, rapidly promoted.

They knew some members of my family, and my father by reputation, and I, of course knew some of theirs, Ireland being such a little country that everyone has some acquaintances in common. They were extremely hospitable, particularly to any of their fellow-countrymen they chanced to meet.

'Deirdre,' her mother called, 'come and meet Mr O'Hagan and Mr Evans.'

A girl detached herself from a group to which she had been talking and came over to us and my heart seemed to stop a beat. At first glance she seemed so like Nancy, my childhood sweetheart who had been forced into the unhappy marriage. She had the same tilt to her head, the same humorous eyes, the same devil-may-care air about her. She was, I was to find, cleverer and more sophisticated and probably more attractive. Certainly, though she was not a great beauty I think there was hardly a man who met her in Malaya who was not a little in love with her.

She greeted us and we instantly fell into conversation about home and who we knew and what we had done. We told her about Malaya, where she had just arrived, and talked and laughed and made plans to show her this and that until long after we should have gone home.

Her parents had bought her out East in the aftermath of an unhappy love affair. The young man to whom she had been engaged had been regarded as 'unsuitable' by her mother, who was something of a snob. His main disadvantage, probably, was that he came from the same town as she did, but from the wrong part of it. His parents ran a small tobacconist shop in a slum area, from which he had emerged with a scholarship which took him to college and on to become an accountant, a considerable achievement in the Ireland of those days.

He was, Deirdre told me, bright and attractive, but uncouth in his manners. To make up for his lack of social grace he had developed an I'm-as-good-as-you style and spoke to her mother and argued with her with a brashness that youth was not expected to show to age at that time. They had become engaged while her parents were posted in India and her mother had hurried home to Ireland to put an end to it. What a clash of wills there must have been, for Deirdre was no shrinking violet. But she had been worn down by her mother's disapproval, by the constant denigration of her fiancé, his background and his lack of manners. The boy, seeing his love affair disintegrating, had lost his head.

There were shouting matches, unforgivable things said to her mother, tearful break-ups, reconciliations and then break-ups again. In the end a compromise had been agreed. They would part for a couple of years, while she accompanied her parents to Malaya, then, if they still wished, they would marry. Even years later, when Deirdre told me the story, I couldn't but feel sorry for him. What hope had he of holding on to her, half a world away? Eventually he married someone else, had a large family and became a wealthy man. Did he ever yearn for his lost love? Would he, or she, have been better off than with the spouses they eventually ended up with? There can be no real answer. Deirdre had loved him greatly, I think, but time cures all, even if it leaves scars sometimes.

Meanwhile, she was far from the land where her young hero slept, and lovers around her were sighing.

'Isn't she wonderful?' said Tommy to me as we drove home.

'Yes,' I said, and the vehemence of my reply caused him to give me a momentary surprised look. 'Much better than your usual,' I added, covering things up.

For, truth to tell, I was as taken by her as he was. So were others. Half the young men in KL seemed to be beating a path to her door. There was a young RAF officer in particular whom her mother greatly favoured, the son of a great English family, titled and a Catholic to boot. There were soldiers and sailors, planters, MCS men and doctors.

She'd say, laughingly: 'My father treats me as if we were still in Victorian times. He insists on me being in by eleven and, if I'm not, he stays up for me. One night the car broke down, and after they spent an hour trying to fix it this nice young officer who hadn't even been with me drove me home out of the kindness of his heart. When we arrived Daddy was waiting for us and tore the poor fellow apart. The only ones he trusts me with are the Irish, and, of course, they're the worst of all!'

Perhaps it was because we were Irish, but we three went everywhere. Tommy was in love as I had never seen him, completely infatuated. The Charleses, the Dereks, the Malcolms and the Richards brought her dancing, plied her with flowers and gifts, but got no further. Even the titled RAF man, despite her mother's best efforts, and no doubt prayers, was gradually dropped.

I seemed to be included in any outings that were being made. I made my excuses, not wishing to be odd man out, but Deirdre always seemed to want to have me along and Tommy, though privately he might have liked more time alone with her, voiced no objections.

Truth to tell I was in a spot, for I was as fascinated by her as he was. I was engaged to be married, I was spoken for, everyone took that for granted. I was in love with Eileen, I was happy, yet I couldn't get Deirdre out of my mind. It was a constant struggle within me, guilt for my secret lack of faithfulness not only to my fiancée but to my closest friend. Not that I ever told anybody. It remained a secret, locked inside me, I thought. Some secret! Deirdre, certainly, knew about it in the way a woman will always know if a man finds her more than usually attractive. Tommy? No, I don't think he ever knew, thank God.

Meanwhile he plied her with presents, sought her company every moment he could and eventually declared his love. She was slow to respond, partly I suppose because the feelings of her last love affair weren't altogether dead, partly because fond though she was of him, she wasn't really in love.

There was a major drawback, too. Tommy was not a Catholic and in those days that mattered greatly. Deirdre's mother, for all her disapproval of her previous entanglement, was as pious as most middle-aged Irish-women were in those days and a marriage to a Prot-estant was definitely to be discouraged. Indeed Tommy's own family would have been every bit as disapproving on their side. Both sides would have worried about which religion the children of a mixed marriage would be brought up in, who would perform the wedding, and whether one or the other of the parties would be in danger of losing their faith.

Ridiculous, you may think today. After all, nine out of ten of the McKennas' friends and colleagues would have been Protestant. But this was a time, remember, before we had ever heard the word ecumenism, when despite personal friendships, marriage between Papist and Prod was still frowned upon. Outside the Catholic Church, we had learned in our catechism that there was no redemption, while on the other side of the divide the old mistrust, hatred indeed, of Romanism, though dying, still held out in many places and ways.

Tommy, he told me, was quietly taken aside and it was suggested to him that he should not get too closely involved with the girl, who was (need one say more?) an RC. He was, however, too head-over-heels in love to care. And all this opposition, in the end, turned out to be a positive advantage, for it turned Deirde towards him with a warmth she had not felt before. Seeing herself about to be thwarted again in her relationship with a man, she dug in her heels and refused to be moved. Her mother, for her part, despite her reservations was unable or unwilling to fight another battle on this ground. Tommy was young, bright and personable, with a good career in front of him – everything, in fact, was in his favour except for his religion. Besides, what would be the result if, yet again, there was a break-up of her daughter's romantic life?

For Christmas we all went to Cameron Highlands, one of the hill stations which had been developed as holiday resorts for Europeans. Here, in the cooler higher altitudes, formerly the jungle haunts of aboriginal tribes who lived a simple, strange nomadic life of hunting, crop-cultivation and a religion based on the interpretation of dreams, little Englands had been carved out. Roses grew around the doors of mock-Tudor cottages, tea rooms served hot buttered scones and, where once the tiger, panther and monkey had prowled, figures in plus-fours putted and drove on immaculately kept golf courses.

In the blessedly cooler air we put on pullovers at night and rejoiced in sitting beside log fires, though in fact it was still as warm as a good summer at home. All around us the hills were covered in jungle, mist-covered in the mornings and by night resounding to the alien whoops and cries of another world. But in our snug little existence we sang Christmas carols, danced to the music of a gramophone, played cards and charades and dreamed of home. Ridiculous Irish-American songs, 'When Irish Eyes Are Smiling', 'How Can You Buy Killarney?' were enough to fill our eyes with sentimental tears as we dreamed of our lost child-hoods and idealized the places that would never be home to us again. Inishfallen, fare thee well!

One day a party of us went for a jungle walk, a gentle enough stroll through well-marked paths on the fringes of the enormous forests. Tommy, for once, wasn't with us, he had a golf match or something, I seem to remember. We set out, six or seven of us together, but on the twisting paths and in the heat we soon got strung out. Deirdre and I found ourselves some way behind the others and I decided we could take a short cut, going down a little-used path that would cut a couple of miles off our route.

It was foolishness of a high order. What made me do it? Did I want to be alone with Deirdre for a bit longer? Foolishness. The path was narrow, it got nar-rower and harder to find. Was there a path there at all? We should have turned back, but by the time we decided to do so it was too late. We were lost. I thought I knew which direction we had come from, but in that tangled wilderness, pushing our way past bushes, twisting and turning, we soon lost all sense of which way we had come. The heat was suffocating, we were covered in sweat and became dreadfully thirsty. Like everyone, though we never mentioned it to each other, we had heard stories of people who had gone into the jungle and never been seen again.

We stopped. I knew that, above all, I had to keep

my head and I tried to think what we should do. Deirdre was getting tired but was admirably composed still. At least, I thought if the worst came to the worst, we weren't deep in the jungle and couldn't be far from help when we were found to be missing. Still, the thought of spending the night in those eerie suroundings, with God knows what prowling around, filled me with dread. In its time the jungle had inspired me, overawed me and horrified me, but I don't think it ever frightened me in the way it did that evening.

I worked out that if we found a stream we could follow its course and, sooner or later it would take us out. As I could think of nothing better we started to walk. But we couldn't find a trace of even the smallest brook, not a trickle. The day was starting to wane and in the depths of the forest it was getting dark already. The undergrowth was so thick that we couldn't see more than about six feet ahead of us. Branches clawed at us, roots tripped us. We had long since stopped talking and were so tired we could hardly walk.

I was just contemplating finding the best spot we could stop and sitting down to wait for help when Deirdre gave a cry. 'Look.' There was more light ahead, the trees were thinning and giving way to long grass and smaller bushes.

We had emerged on the side of a hill, planted with tea bushes. Down through it ran a small stream, which must have been less than a hundred yards from where we had been stumbling through the jungle. We crouched beside it, sweat-stained and dirty, almost crying with relief and plunged our faces into the water, drinking deep. Satiated we sat on the ground, breathing deeply. Our hands brushed and I took hers, then my arms were around her and we were, for a moment, kissing.

'No, Tim,' she said. 'No!'

We broke apart. I looked into her face. It was now or never, some sort of turning point.

'I'm very sorry,' I said. 'I don't know what . . .' The words died away.

A silence fell. The jungle chorus behind us started up.

'Come on,' she said. 'It's time we were getting home.'

Once more I avoided the point of confrontation. We never spoke of the episode again.

They were married six months later in the Catholic cathedral in KL. Faced with the inevitable, Deirdre's mother finally capitulated and, for his part, Tommy agreed to the conditions laid down by the Catholic Church for mixed marriages, so-called. The wedding was quite an occasion. The bride's sister came all the way from Ireland to act as bridesmaid, there was a military guard of honour outside the church for the colonel's daughter, uniforms and decorations all over the shop, and the Governor himself came up for the ceremony. The parents of the bride hosted a reception for a large assembly of guests in their home afterwards. Deirdre was more beautiful than ever in her white dress, Tommy was everything a fine young man should be. And, oh, yes, the best man was Mr Tim O'Hagan, a school friend of the bridegroom's, now, like him, a member of the Malayan Civil Service. Due to be married himself, we hear, when he returns to Ireland later this year at the end of his first three-year term of service.

What thoughts were in Deirdre's mind that day? Her lost love in Ireland? Tommy? Me, even? Did she realize that, in the lottery of marriage, she had drawn a winning ticket? Nobody can ever really know what goes on in the secret depths of a long-lasting relationship between a man and a woman, except the pair themselves. But to all appearances and, knowing them better than anybody, I think I can safely say that this was a pairing, as the cliché goes, made in heaven. Her humour, gregariousness and zest for life lightened and drew out his shyness and conservatism, while his steadfastness and palpable adoration of her steadied a temperament that could descend from the heights of fun into black pits of depression. Through the years their love for each other deepened and grew until death parted them. How bloody lucky they were!

Chapter Five

AFTER THREE years I returned to Ireland and my first leave. How strange and yet familiar it all seemed to me, how cold, how grey, how green, how beautiful! The world and my native land had changed, of course, since I left. The Great War had taken its toll, a new independent country ruled by new men was in the process of being born, the old order was passing. Violence was the order of the day. The old parliamentary way of doing things was over, the clubby collusion with Westminster politicians had been undone by the executions of 1916. There were marchings and drillings, secret landings of arms, outrages in country lanes. The Black and Tan war, the civil war, the partition of the island and the bourgeois Church-dominated Free State were all just around the corner.

If we could have seen the new Ireland that was coming, reactionary, priest-ridden, full of sterile anti-British feeling, economically and politically backward, how many of us would have settled for it? Of course, neither the country's leaders nor the mass of its citizens saw it that way. Despite the massive emigration, unemployment and poverty, the petty-mindedness and the puritanism, most Irishmen and women thought of themselves as living in the greatest little country in the world, a beacon of Christian life surrounding godless wickedness.

The political changes seemed to me to make little impact on the comfortable life of my family and friends. Not surprisingly, for, despite independence, the middle classes were as comfortably unchallenged as ever they had been under British rule. My brother Mick, it is true, had fallen in the war just before I left for the East, while my brothers Harry and Johnny were by now off in America and China respectively. My other brothers and sisters (we were a large family) went about their lives, much as they had done when I left.

My father, grown old-looking, was still a man to be feared and respected, though my own manhood had made me a little less in awe of him. Still a power in the community, his political views had, inevitably, the whiff of a past generation.

My mother ... How does a man describe his mother? A quiet woman, not given, you might think, to many displays of emotion, though I have seen her weep at deaths and I know she worried about us all in the various difficulties and dramas of our lives. She went about her work on the farm, correct in everything she did, undemonstrative in the country way, yet always loving. Do I idealize her? All I know is that my heart leaped to see her again.

The business of our family farm was still the same, too. The crops were harvested, the cattle were milked, butter was churned, the same people came and went, the same pony pulled the same trap when we went in and out of town, the same dogs greeted me with the same rapture.

The middle classes of Ireland still played rugby football, as they do to this day, golfed and shot and fished, met in the evenings to chatter and play cards or sing. Nothing disturbed the tenor of their comfortable, conservative lives. There were arguments, of course, about politics. Most were in favour of independence, but few enough were prepared to do more than vote for it.

The country was 'up', as they say. Violent nationalism was having one of those periods of popularity which occur cyclically in our history and new voices were being heard. The Black and Tan war, or 'War of Independence' to give it its grander title, was being fought for the most part by small farmers, artisans and unskilled labourers, the men of no property. They were imprisoned, killed and were killed for a 'freedom' that differed very little from what had gone before, or so it seemed to me. When independence came, if they were perspicacious enough, they would realize little had changed. There were ambushes, burnings, atrocities and, when it was over, the victors turned on each other and fought a civil war over the treaty that had been signed with Britain. But, as wars go, these were small ones, and it's surprising in retrospect how little effect it all had on the humdrum settled existence of most of the bourgeoisie. Ever thus, you'll say.

My life was pleasant beyond belief. As a traveller from the far side of the world, at a time when not many had been much further afield than Dublin, I was an object of intense curiosity – something of a hero, even. I had returned from an impossibly remote place where, they seemed to think, I led a life of glamour and danger, a life where adventures were a daily occurrence. Unlike later, when I had lost touch with most of my college friends one by one, they were nearly all still eager to invite me everywhere. Because I was officially on leave my father didn't expect me to work, barring the occasional task which I gladly carried out at home, and I had, by the modest standards of the time, plenty of money.

The local paper even ran a short piece about me, headed 'An Irishman in Malaya' . . . 'Third son of the well-known Mr Terence O'Hagan . . . just returned from the Malay States, where he holds a senior position in the Colonial Civil Service . . . says it is a beautiful country . . . friendly natives . . . extensive areas of jungle . . . shot a wild boar . . . graduate with first class honours of Queen's College . . . engaged to a County Limerick lady, Miss Eileen Casey . . .'

Of course the main purpose of my return was Eileen, to meet her again, to see what we still felt for each other and, all being well, to carry her off as my bride.

My secret love for Deirdre had shaken my confidence in what I felt for Eileen, but with the resilience of the young I had half forgotten the episode, refused to make a drama out of it and got on with my life. What would have been the point? Now, though, a decision of some sort would have to be made. At first it was as if we were strangers. There were aching silences between us, moments when we seemed to have nothing left to say to each other. She had worked as a teacher in my absence and her talk was of the convent school where she taught, of her family and her world, while mine was of far horizons, strange peoples and exotic flora and fauna.

When I told her, suitably censored, of my visit to Campbell she was horrified, shocked by his immorality, bewildered by his way of life. But all she said, perhaps with some reason, was: 'He must be mad.' For my part, my head probably a bit turned by my own legend, her talk of engagements and dresses and her parents' shortcomings seemed insufferably dull and provincial.

Yet there was never a moment when we questioned out loud the inevitability of our marriage. It was an age, remember, when people didn't examine themselves and their affairs half as minutely as they do today. We were engaged, our respective families approved, to break it up would have been a calamity of inconceivable proportions . . . and I don't think we ever seriously considered it.

I suppose if we had been very level-headed, wise and careful we would have asked ourselves how things might work out. It was, after all, a big step to take an inexperienced young woman more than six thousand miles away to a very strange country where she would not know a single soul apart from myself and Tommy, where she would have to put up with a trying climate and intense loneliness. But I had seen other young women do the same, go through all that and yet, like myself, come to love Malaya and its peoples. My head was turned by the place and I was sure, I was certain, that she would come to share my enthusiasm.

Perhaps she is the one who should have cried halt, but that would probably have been impossible for her, too. She had more steel in her than might at first be apparent, but to jilt me would have required a strong-mindedness, and a certainty about herself and what she was doing that at that time and that age few of us possessed. One can imagine the scenes if she had tried, her ghastly mother and her awful father erupting like twin volcanoes, the talk in the town, always a major consideration, and, of course, the hurt and the shattered incomprehension with which I would have greeted it! No, if in some secret corner of her heart there were doubts, they were never allowed to surface.

And I was in love with her again, falling once more as I had before, forgetting what had gone between. I loved her gentleness, I loved the delicacy of her face, the grace of her movements. It flattered me that she seemed to defer to me, something which few people had ever done. I rejoiced in her beauty, it seemed to me that all the world was smiling on me.

Our first awkwardness with each other didn't last long. There was a blissful month in West Clare, swimming, boating, walking the open springy headlands, with the huge blue seas of the Irish West crashing on the rocks below and the wind warm and salt-laden in our faces.

We walked over those wonderful cliffs, the sea birds flying hundreds of feet below us. In winter, great slabs crashed into the wild ocean, leaving huge bridges of rock spanning chasms where the sea boiled and echoed, or an ancient castle perched precariously on a headland, or a tiny church, once the praying place of anchorites, marooned on an island that rose three hundred feet straight out of the waves. We stole occasional kisses when we escaped the not too intense watchfulness of her maiden aunt or whoever was allegedly chaperoning us. We held hands, we gazed at each other. Once – innocent times – I put a hand on her breast, she blushed hotly and turned away.

When she wasn't there my brothers and friends golfed or went to swim in the cold exhilarating waters of the Atlantic, off great beaches or in big pools left by the tides. In those days the best places were for men only, and the solid burghers and parish priests of Limerick sunned themselves on the flat rocks like pink and white walruses. I can remember a couple of unfortunate English ladies who didn't know the local customs straying to one such place.

'Ladies,' said a portly canon, his towel round him like a toga, 'have you lost something?'

'Why, no, Father.'

'Yiz have! Yiz have lost your modesty!'

Withdrawal in confusion. Hilarity, pomposity, all round.

At night we would attend a play, performed by Anew McMaster's touring company: *Othello*; *Sweeney Todd, the Demon Barber*; *The Life and Death of Lord Edward Fitzgerald*, a wide repertoire. ''Twas very well done . . .' 'I thought, apart from McMaster, they were poor enough . . .' Otherwise we danced, and round a piano sang Victorian drawing-room ballads of blighted love or the sentimental, humorous songs of Percy French so beloved of the Irish, or played for ha'pennies, forty-five, a hundred and ten, those complicated card games of Munster.

Our wedding and honeymoon were to take place just before my, or rather our, return to Malaya. When I think of it now I realize with what dread she must have looked forward to it, to leaving her comfortable world, to going to what she thought of as a hostile wilderness without friends or relations, to entrusting herself to me. But I was so blinded, both by my love for her and my growing obsession with Malaya, which I was certain she would come to share, that I paid no attention to her fears, or belittled them.

We were married in the autumn by my brother Johnny, Father Johnny, an austere young priest whose reactionary views were, if anything, to be hardened by twenty years' toil amongst the Heathen Chinee. The Caseys had put out the boat for the big day, sparing no expense. Her father wore a new, somewhat loud suit, his bull neck almost bursting out of the hard collar that surrounded it, her mother was resplendent in the fur of some large dead animal, from which came the reek of mothballs. Everyone was there, including my distant cousin the Bishop, something which caused my new in-laws almost to burst with pride and to bore their neighbours nearly to extinction for months afterwards with their name-dropping.

My best man was one of my brothers, Tommy being still in Malaya. He made a halting speech, followed by one from the father of the bride, who had been coached within an inch of his life in what to say by a wife fearful that he would let down the family honour by some dreadful omission or crudity. Trammelled by his strangulating collar and refusing so much as a single whiskey in case it might loosen his coarse tongue, he spoke woodenly and, mercifully, briefly. My own father, who followed, had no such problems. He spoke with the fluency of a man well used to addressing the public, said all the right things and gave me indications of a love he had for me and a pride in what I had done which, in our way, he had never spoken of to me personally.

I followed. Though I have been forced to do my fair share of it, public speaking is not one of my gifts. I hear my own voice coming back at me and always feel it is inadequate. But on this occasion I surpassed myself. I was witty, I was to the point. People laughed at my jokes, applauded my tributes to family and friends, clapped me on the back when I had finished. Quite the golden-tongued orator.

After me came his Grace the Bishop who spoke (what else?) of the glories of Christian (for which read Catholic) marriage. He was listened to with a respect which the commonality of his remarks hardly merited, and scandalized cries of 'Shhh!' broke out when one of the guests who had drunk too much (there's always one, isn't there?) kept talking to his neighbour through the speech and then knocked over a glass with a crash.

In short, it was a very typical wedding.

We were driven away, our shoulders spattered with rice, to our honeymoon in Glendalough, then a remote valley of particularly melancholy beauty in the Wicklow mountains. It was autumn, damp and dark, and we had the hotel to ourselves except for an English couple on some sort of walking holiday. An elderly boots doubled as barman, a similarly ageing maid served us indifferent food. By day we walked among the heather and the ruins of the early monastic settlement which had stood there more than a millennium before. Surely those early Irish monks must have had their flesh mortified, not just by prayer, fasting and Viking raiders, but by unremitting rheumatism. High on a cliff overlooking one of the lakes was St Kevin's Bed, which legend had it was a cell to which the saint who had founded the settlement used to retire for solitary prayer and self-abnegation. Here he had been visited by a local damsel who had fallen in love with him and who was anxious to offer him her favours. But the saint, a good Irish cleric if ever there was one, had avoided temptation by hurling her into the waters far below, an early example of the order of priorities of a Church to which homicide has always seemed less culpable than fornication.

In the evening we read books in a lounge decorated with hunting prints and stuffed specimen fish and, in our bedroom after three days in which nothing at all happened between us, we consummated our marriage. At first, I would kiss her and hold her in our bed, but as soon as I became aroused she would turn from me with a whispered 'good night', leaving me frustrated and wakeful. On the third night in that sodden valley, my impatience got the better of me, I lay on top of her and entered her. She did not try to prevent me, God help her. How clumsy I must have been, how insensitive, for I felt it was my right, indeed my duty to have sexual intercourse with my wife. I have regretted that night a thousand times. Intercourse, intercurse, the tyranny of the bed, the need to prove oneself.

Perhaps because of this bad beginning, our sexual life was never easy. I don't know what she had been told about the marriage bed, little enough I am sure. For my part I knew nothing at all beyond what I had gleaned from reading and my sole experience dipping into Campbell's sleeping dictionary on the rubber estate that night.

In that Ireland where every erotic spasm, every adolescent masturbatory fantasy was a 'bad thought' that could condemn you to everlasting hell-fire, sexuality and guilt became inextricably mixed. It was recognized that such things existed, but as dark evils, the work of the devil who wanted us all to roast. What one mustn't do was 'take pleasure in it' and for many celibate priests and nuns it must have ben a life-long struggle and one that obsessed them to the point where no other sin really existed. Even those of us who were married found that our sexual lives within the sacrament were circumscribed and confined, and regarded as somehow or other a necessary evil. Some escaped this feeling, of course, but many must have entered the marriage bed wearing an invisible crown of thorns. Certainly our own pairing was, even when things were going well, a stop-go affair, something we never discussed but somehow less than it should have been.

On a grey October evening we left Dun Laoghaire

on the mail boat which would bring us to Liverpool and the liner which would take us to the Far East. Eileen's parents were there to see her off and she clung to them, most uncharacteristically, while I fussed about the numerous bags, tin trunks and other bits of luggage which accompanied one on long voyages in those days.

Standing forlornly on the pier, waiting to embark, her face was white. It was clearly a nightmare for her. The bustle of embarkation went on around our little group. She promised to write, her mother promised to write, her father attempted some gruff jokes, prompting the usual glare from her mother. My own feelings were mixed. I knew that a golden chapter in my life was ending, but was certain that another was about to begin. Then it was time to go and her face was wet with tears. We stood on deck, my arm around her, looking back on the vanishing lights of Dublin Bay and for her it must have been as if the worst had happened.

At Liverpool we changed into the bigger and grander P&O liner. Old friends greeted each other on board, there were people I knew, a general atmosphere of bonhomie, high good humour, a pretence maybe to hide the homesickness that so many felt. In the days that followed Eileen became silent and withdrawn and matters weren't helped by a particularly miserable crossing of the Bay of Biscay, during which nearly everybody aboard was sick all the time.

When we entered the Mediterranean things got better, as they always do when the sun starts to shine. Life aboard ship was friendly and easy-going. People pay large sums of money nowadays for just the sort of thing that was part of going and coming from the East then. Deck games, a shipboard swimming pool, dinner and dancing, fancy dress parties, and flirtations for the unmarried, and some of the married too. Eileen, looking wonderfully pretty in summer dresses, made friends with other young women, received all sorts of compliments and thoroughly enjoyed it.

The East began, of course, not at ever-so-British Gibraltar, but at the other end of the Mediterranean at Port Said and the Suez Canal. I noticed some of Eileen's alarm returning as she surveyed the squalid dockside, with its intense heat, flies and noise, and the unceasingly importunate vendors of everything from carpets to boxes of Turkish Delight which, when opened, turned out to have been packed with camel dung.

But Port Said was a very different place to Malaya and I thought her spirits would rise again. On we sailed, Aden, Bombay, Ceylon, days too hot to do anything but lie around and watch the flying fish that skimmed along with us, cooler starlit nights when the sea shone with phosporescence. On the P&O ships they blew a bugle to announce dinner and the Indian army officers would appear in their splendid dress uniforms. The rest of us wore, of course, black tie and dinner jackets, something many were to continue to do in the remotest jungles and deserts of the Empire on which the sun never . . . etc, thereby in some peculiar way asserting our superiority over those who actually clad themselves to suit the climate. After dinner it was cards and dancing, and, of course, more drinks – though we might never meet again, we were the closest of friends for those few weeks.

India and Ceylon came and went, and in each we lost some of the passengers, so that our complement was well down as we headed ever further east. The presence of Malaya became apparent even before we sighted land. The extraordinary colour of the sea, almost oily in its calmness, the wonderful sight of a school of dolphins swimming just below the surface beside our ship, the smell of blossoms, cloves and God knows what else which Conrad calls 'the first sigh of the East on my face'.

We passed a Chinese junk. Then, at last, the sight of land, the island of Penang dominated by its tall hill. Blue outlines became defined, we passed beaches and bays surrounded everywhere by ever-encroaching greenery, fishing villages on stilts, and then came the port with its thousand porters and peddlers, its rickshaws, its Chinese bazaars.

Down on the quayside someone was waving. It was Tommy and Deirdre, each in white, each brown and healthy-looking. We were all together, so happy to see each other, laughing, swapping news of home and Malaya. Deirdre was beautiful, contented and pregnant. Our eyes met. She smiled and gave me a squeeze, no more, then she carried Eileen off with her.

Often now at night I dream – or, perhaps I should say, often now I remember in my dreams. People come to me there, often people whom I do not know. Who can they be, these dream people? Sometimes, though, people I know well come to me too. Tommy, Eileen, Deirdre, others. They say things to me but they make no sense. Could there be a meaning, a key? The interpretation of dreams – must look it up.

I have a picture in my head. A dream? No, I think it happened. Eileen is standing on the edge of a *padang*, a parade ground. Tall palm trees surround it, and behind them are those handsome, white, vaguely Moorish buildings that will probably be the last legacy of British rule in Malaya. Whiteness is the order of the day. On the grass, where inevitably a football or hockey pitch is marked out, a band in white ducks and pith helmets plays excerpts from Gilbert and Sullivan: 'A wand'ring minstrel I, a thing of shreds and patches . . .', 'I have a song to sing you, Sing me your song-oh . . .'

She is young, she is pretty, she smiles. Ladies with parasols sit around, men in white. The wind sighs in the trees, servants bring cool drinks. Life is easy. Beyond, never far away, lies the immensity, the mystery of the jungle, the mountains, the coral-rimmed islands.

'So what do you make of Malaya, Mrs O'Hagan?' someone asks.

'It seems very nice, I suppose,' she answers politely.

Chapter Six

IN HIS *Golden Bough* Fraser writes of a peculiar
Malay ceremony connected with the durian tree,
which often shoots up to a height of eighty or ninety
feet without putting out a branch. Near a place called
Jugra, in Selangor, he says, there is a small grove of
durian trees and on a specially chosen day the local
villagers used to assemble in it. Then one of their medicine men would take a hatchet and strike one of the
trees several times, saying: 'Will you bear fruit or not?
If you do not I shall fell you.' Meanwhile another man
would have climbed a mangosteen tree nearby (the
durian tree being unclimbable) and would reply on
behalf of the durian: 'Yes, I will bear fruit. I beg you
not to fell me.'

Our first posting on Eileen's arrival was to KL, the
second city of the area after Singapore, and capital of
the Federated Malay States. As cities go it is not the
most beautiful or interesting, having sprung up towards
the end of the last century at the confluence of a couple
of muddy streams where tin had been found, and offering little in the way of natural splendour. But, in many
ways, it could not have been a better start. There were
plenty of Europeans there, decent places to live and
plenty to do.

Best of all, though, was the presence of Tommy and

Deirdre. We went everywhere together, we four, and life was easy with not too much work, servants to cater for all our domestic needs and few worries about money. There were dinners and picnics, tennis, visits to the swimming pool and parties that lasted into the small hours, after which we would drive by the bright starlight to the Malay quarter and eat the delicious *satays* and other little dishes which were cooking at the open-air stalls that were all over the place.

Once she got over her initial shyness Eileen seemed to settle and a warm friendship grew up between herself and Deirdre. But she suffered a martyrdom of homesickness for Ireland and her awful parents, and there were other signs that Malaya was not for her. She went through agonies with the climate, her fair skin turning an angry pink, tortured by prickly heat and bumps and itches. The voracious insect life of the peninsula seemed to find her the most appetizing of meals. They say that mosquitoes, in particular, prefer the blood of someone fresh out from Europe, who has not yet had the chance to build up whatever the substance is that they dislike in the blood of natives. She was, anyway, bitten and stung by flies and beetles, by ants and creatures which I couldn't even classify.

It was expected that *mems* would learn the language, or at any rate a sort of pidgin Malay, or even a few key words and phrases. But she made no attempt to do so and was thus constantly at cross-purposes with the servants, though their elementary English was at least better than her non-existent Malay.

One day I arrived home to find her in hysterics. A rather small snake had slithered across the floor of our living room while she was reading a magazine. Our *sais*, Kassim, had come to the rescue promptly and cut the creature's head off with a gardening spade. He regarded the episode as a source of huge merriment, but Eileen took to her bed and had nightmares, she told me, for a week. A picnic to the fringes of the jungle with the Evanses was not a success either. She found the steamy heat intolerable, the pullulating vegetation claustrophobic and the occasional distant yelp of a monkey a source of alarm. She said she couldn't breathe and we were forced to go home early.

After a year our first child was born – a boy whom we called Maurice. As we were still in KL Eileen was able to enter a decent hospital, not like some places in the outback where you had to have someone pour a bucket of water through a hole in the roof when you wanted a shower. It was a difficult birth, but the doctor was wonderful – one of those ultra-competent, pipe-smoking Englishmen. I thought he was a stuffed shirt, but he surrounded himself with an aura of calm authority that made his women patients adore him.

The baby was fine, but Eileen was shattered. It was as if she didn't want to know him, as if he was responsible for the pain and the fear she'd gone through – he and Malaya, a country she increasingly blamed for everything, from the climate to her twenty-four-hour labour. She spent much of the day lying on her bed, often refusing to talk to me for no reason, reading an unending pile of cheap romantic novels or just gazing into space. The highlight of the day was the arrival of the post, with the hope of letters from home, and when there were none, as was inevitably the case most days, she would lapse into gloom again.

Maurice was handed over to an *amah*, a Chinese nursemaid. Thank God for the Chinese *amah*, that spotlessly clean, imperturbable presence, in her starched white jacket and black trousers, who lifted and laid the baby as if he was her own, putting him down at night behind his mosquito nets (no sheets, let alone blankets in that climate), bathing him and washing his clothes so that he was like a small, pink, sweet-smelling parcel.

She took him for walks in his pram and presented him, content and fed, when we wanted him at the start of the day and again at bedtime. Then I would play with him and he would smile up at me, making him seem to me altogether the most wonderful thing that had ever happened. If you're one of those people who is at ease with children your first one is like your first love – you may have others you love just as much, but the intensity of the pleasure will never be the same again.

I think Eileen resented what I felt. Jealousy in part that any other being should take even a part of what I felt for her. It seemed to drive that invisible wedge between us a little bit deeper. Still, she rallied somewhat from her depression, thanks mainly to Deirdre who listened to her complaints, sympathized with her and jollied her out of her introspection, forcing her to go out, meet other women and involve herself again in the social life of the city.

Shortly after that, we were moved from KL to a small town also on the west coast. The mystic East! It was about as exotic as Tullamore or Longford. We lived in a concrete box called a bungalow with an ill-kept garden and, across the road, the inevitable row after row of rubber trees.

The town comprised one dusty street that contained some shops selling bags of rice, baskets of spices, greasy ducks hanging on hooks, luke-warm bottles of beer, tins of paraffin and cheap Japanese toys. There was a basic Chinese-run hotel, with bare-boarded rooms above a shop. There was a market that sold fish and vegetables and scrawny live chickens, whose throats were slit on the spot for the benefit of the customers, whereupon they were plucked, still warm, and delivered with heads and claws intact, these last being considered delicacies.

Most of the stallholders were Chinese or Indian, though there was a separate pork market some distance away, in respect of the Malays' Muslim sensibilities. There was a rest house, a bungalow for peripatetic colonial administrators, run by a gloomy Indian husband and wife. There was a highly coloured Chinese temple, guarded by a spectacularly bad-tempered dog, and an even more garish Hindu one where, on feast days, crowds covered themselves in coloured powders, and some of them stuck skewers through their cheeks and noses, or hooks into their shoulders, with no lasting ill-effects that I could see. The dust rolled around and choked you, except when the rain came lashing down, and then the place flooded. And that more or less exhausted the possibilities of Jalong, except for the Club.

Ah, yes, the Club. The hub of social life for the Europeans of the area. The Club ... sounds quite attractive, doesn't it? There was a worn tennis court, which the inevitable Tamil gardener tended dispiritedly. There was a five-hole golf course (yes, five, don't ask me why) which was in perpetual danger of being swallowed by the ferocious local vegetation. In the midst of this stood another bungalow, surrounded by a verandah to give it shade. There was a small library of well-thumbed books – Agatha Christie, aged copies of *The London Illustrated News* and, of course, Somerset

Maugham. Maugham was at once hated and hero-worshipped in Malaya. He came out, it was said, listened to club anecdotes and transformed them into scurrilous stories, often about recognizable people. Yet, you'd had to admit, didn't you, that he was the greatest living writer, and, after all, he was writing about us.

But back to the Club. Inside, there was a threadbare billiards table and, of course, the bar. The bar. Now you're talking! Here, evening after evening, came the planters and civil servants, the tin miners and police officers and the few wives of the area, to drink *stengahs* and *pahits* and to bore the pants off each other with the same jokes, the same reminiscences, the same back-biting which had been going on for years. Here came Mowbray who had a Chinese wife and, it was rumoured, an English one back home, Woods, who had lived in Australia, Chambers and his wife, who it was said wrote poetry, though no one had ever seen it, Scully, the Irish doctor, of whom more later, Stillman, who had once been involved in fisticuffs with that young chap from the Public Works Department, and all the others with their modest claims to fame.

Occasionally a new face would appear, but basically it was the same small group of people who had been there for what seemed like for ever. Many of them bored, lonely people, forced together by life. The only wonder was that they didn't dislike each other more – not that most of them would ever admit they weren't in the most fascinating of company, nor that they weren't doing the most interesting of jobs in the best of all worlds.

So here we are in Jalong, hub of the universe. With the birth and subsequent trauma, our sexual life had come to a halt and it took a good six months for it to get going again. The birth, the baby, it was as if they were a barrier between us. But something, I can't remember what, got it started again – probably the need to find something to do in the evenings. At any rate we made love again regularly and within a year and a half of Maurice's birth Eileen was pregnant for the second time.

We'd arranged to go back to Kuala Lumpur and Dr Simpson again for the birth, but the baby took us by surprise. If Maurice's birth had been long and hard, this one was easy. Too bloody easy! Two weeks before it was due it decided to make its entrance into the world.

There were two doctors in Jalong, an Indian who was perfectly competent, but whom Eileen wouldn't have because of his dark face, or black as she called it . . . Christ! The other, Scully, a fellow-countryman. I knew him from the Club, where he always greeted me like a long-lost brother.

He smelled in equal parts of whiskey and sweat and had a disreputable career behind him. Time in a Dublin hospital, which he had left in a hurry. Some question, I gather, of incompetence, of malpractice. Why the hell wasn't he just struck off, banned from plying the trade? Give him a last chance, send him abroad, the traditional Irish solution to all mistakes.

He had worked in some back-street practice in the north of England, he told me, for a time (performing illegal abortions, according to club gossip), then served for nearly ten years as a ship's doctor. Not too fussy who they have on some of these boats, rough and ready medicine. Somehow or other he had come to Jalong, where he divided most of his time between the Club and the local drinking shops. He was not well-liked, and not just because his personal odour made it a trial to stand beside him. He had a hail-fellow-well-met air about him when sober that could turn sour and truculent when in his cups. He seemed to feel that life had treated him unfairly and, given half a chance, would pour out bile at Ireland, the medical profession and anything or anyone else with whom he'd come in contact. He had a native mistress, whom I am sure he beat, and after a bottle of whiskey was given to boasting about the patients he had killed in his time – most of them unfortunate Chinese coolies who could afford no better.

I was summoned from my office by a messenger to say that Eileen had gone into labour and I hurried home. I suggested we get the Indian doctor but Eileen would have none of it.

'Get Scully,' she said.

'But, really, do you think he's the best?'

'Get him,' she said, 'get him! Hurry!'

There was no arguing with her at that point, so I sent Kassim with word to come immediately. Time passed. No Scully. Kassim returned. Had he given the message? Yes. He shrugged. It told me everything.

Eileen was crying with pain.

Amah took over. Calmly and expertly she delivered a healthy five-pound girl – my daughter. When it was all over and mother and baby slept Scully arrived, looking as if he'd slept in his clothes.

'Sorry, old boy,' he said. 'Held up on a case. Everything all right?'

If Eileen had resented her first-born, she greeted this baby with a fierce all-consuming joy that frightened me even then. It was too much, too possessive, too all-consuming. She would gaze at the little girl for hours, dress her and feed her and lift her, and could hardly bear to be out of her presence for half an hour. Even *amah*, who was better with children than Eileen ever would be, was hardly allowed to touch her.

What a beauty she was, the little *mem*, my little daughter! She was so . . . so neat. Tiny, but put together like an older child. Brown . . . brown curls . . . gold curls . . . What did she look like? I remember her toddling beside me, holding my hand, so small beside me. She started to walk very early on. Everyone used to smile at her. The *sais*, the number one boy, the number two boy, cookie, the gardener, they'd smile when they saw her holding my hand.

What was it killed her, now? Typhoid, yellow fever, cholera, dengue fever, malaria? There were so many diseases then, all child-killers. That's why we sent them home so early, so indecently young, to the cold comfort of boarding schools in Europe.

She had become sick, she had a temperature. We sent for Scully, eventually he arrived – a brief interlude in his love affair with the bottle. He greeted me, as ever, like a brother, a fellow-exile of Erin. He was keen to get the medical side of things over with as soon as possible and get to the production of the whiskey bottle, the banal talk of home (he was, I remember, a great admirer of Mr de Valera). Meanwhile he took a more or less cursory look at the sick baby. A fever, minor, nothing to worry about, be over in a day or two, take this, call in again tomorrow.

I remember the cot with the mosquito nets around it. Eileen sitting beside it, all day, all night. Not eating, not sleeping, wiping the small sweating face with a damp cloth. That small face, what was it *like*? White, white. Quiet. No crying. No whimpering. The

95

breathing . . . the breathing, I remember, got laboured, whistling . . . Jesus. She wasn't even two.

I went over to collect Scully in my car. He lived in another undistinguished bungalow. It was dingy, dilapidated, it smelled of him. A middle-aged Chinese woman with a pudgy face and dead eyes answered my knock, the mistress I suppose.

'He no here,' she said in response to my enquiry.

'Where is he?' I asked. 'It's a matter of urgency.'

'I no know. I tell when he come back.'

As I turned to go Scully came into the room. He was unshaved, dressed in a sweat-stained vest and a pyjama bottom. He was on a bender.

'Tim!' he cried. 'Always a pleasure to see a fellow-Irishman. Here, have a drink.' He had a whiskey bottle in his hand. 'Get him a glass, *cepat*,' he ordered the Chinawoman.

'No,' I said, 'some other time.'

'What's up? Is it the kid?' he asked. He took a few steps forward, staggered and saved himself from falling by holding on to a table.

'It's all right,' I said. 'Some other time.'

His bonhomie vanished. 'Whadda you mean, all right?' he said. 'I want to know about my patient. Whadda you mean "*awl* right"?', making it sound posh and pompous to mock me.

'Cheerio, be in touch,' I said, turning to go.

I went out and back to the car.

He clawed his way out on to the verandah after me.

'Fucking stuck-up MCS,' he shouted after me. 'Fucking pompous shit!'

The Chinese woman tried to take him by the arm and lead him back inside. He swung his elbow angrily behind him, catching her on the side of the face. I drove away.

Jesus Christ, I could have killed him. I should have killed him . . . What would have been the point? He was dead anyway within a month, from a massive heart attack after one of his drinking sprees.

I got the young Indian doctor. 'I am most sorry to tell you, sir, that this child is dying. There is nothing that can be done.'

Eileen, who had behaved so (what shall I say?) heroically until then, went berserk. She screamed, she tore her clothes. She cursed the country and the doctor and the *amah*. She used language so foul that I would never have dreamed in a hundred years she even knew the words. I had to pin her down; the doctor gave her a draught of something that calmed her and we put her to bed. Whatever it was it must have knocked her cold.

'*Tuan, tuan.*' *Amah* was calling me. Whoever says the Chinese are inscrutable is a bloody fool. There were tears pouring down her face. The breathing had stopped from the cot . . .

There are gaps . . . there are gaps. I remember a funeral. Cars driving up. Women dabbing their eyes, men looking grave. Handshakes. Prayers. The Catholics kneeling and sitting and standing, the others not knowing quite what to do. A French priest; I didn't like him much, why I can't remember. It's funny, you remember the dislike, not the reasons for it. There was a small white coffin – it seemed, somehow, indecent. There were some words. 'May her soul and the souls of all the faithful departed rest in . . .' Was Eileen there, or was she sedated, stunned in some shaded room while it all went on? I can't remember . . . Or am I thinking of some other funeral of some other child?

I went back to Jalong many years later and I went to the churchyard. There it was, beautifully kept: 'Patricia, aged one-and-a-half years, to the unending grief of her parents, Tim and Eileen O'Hagan. Mother of Perpetual Succour pray for us.' All around her were other casualties of Empire, many of them children too, sometimes two or three of the same family cut down by a disease. There they lay in their trim graves, far from the native lands which most of them had never seen, resting their eternal rests beneath the leaves like shields, the thrusting grasses that would cover their stones and envelop all traces of them if it were not for the unceasing efforts of some underpaid gardener.

A hundred yards away, at the other end of the church grounds, was another set of names cut into stone. These marked the resting places of still another set of exiles – part of the diasporas of the great cities, hills and plains of India and China. Yes, here lay the Asiatic converts of the good fathers. Mr Woo and Mr Singh and all their families, who had embraced the Faith that came from the West. They had honoured God and served the king, said their rosaries, confessed their sins, struggled with the difficult and often inexplicable precepts of salvation, like us all, with varying degrees of success.

Fine people, pious people, but even in death they could not lie beside the masters of Empire. Even in Paradise there must be some dissatisfied souls. I mean, what would the *memsahibs*, who fought so long and so hard to keep black, brown and yellow faces out of the clubs of Malaya, think if they found heaven full of those lesser breeds – always assuming those haughty ladies had arrived there themselves. Or maybe it's been better arranged up there. Something like Malaya, in fact. Clubs for Europeans, clubs for Chinese, clubs for Malays. In my Father's house there are many mansions . . .

So that's how I lost my only daughter and, as it transpired, my wife and son as well. Our hearts were broken, both of us, but there was a difference. I was a young man, interested in my life, happy in the place fate had dropped me, and, I suppose, like young men everywhere I was capable of getting over just about anything. But Eileen's heartbreak seemed to be without end, bottomless and inconsolable. Her consolation was prayer. She went every day to mass, she spent hours on her knees, but her nights were punctuated by wild outbursts of crying and terrible screams of pain.

My heart was bleeding for the death of the baby and even more for her agony. But life went on for me. I worked, I met people, I travelled round the state. Inevitably it took my mind off things, while she stayed at home in her anguish. I was unable to match the intensity of her grief. This she knew and she blamed me for it. I didn't care, I was callous. When I would tell her – how banal it sounded – that time would heal her pain, she would round on me angrily. She didn't wish her pain to end, I was unfeeling, I cared about nothing but myself, her life was at an end anyway, so what did it matter? Anything could set her off, the sight of a child, a visit to the cinema, something she'd read or even some chance remark somebody would make.

Weeks passed, months passed and it got no better. I started to resent it. I blame myself for that. It was heartless of me. It was . . . impatient. I would come home after work, she would be still in bed, not having got up all day.

'This has to stop,' I would say. 'Life has to go on, it's intolerable.'

She would say nothing, gaze at me stonily in that bedroom with the blinds drawn. Pull a sheet over her head.

I'd go out, pace up and down. Eat a meal by myself. I resented the fact that I couldn't even express my own grief, because so much of the time was taken up with fruitlessly trying to console hers. Her state was becoming more important than the child's death, I would tell myself.

This would go on for hours. Then I would return to the room and apologize for my behaviour. Apologize for wrongs I had not committed. It made no difference. The same stony stare, the same silence.

I seemed to be moving back and forth between grief and anger and apology. That was the first time I started to drink heavily, emptying the whiskey bottle before falling into bed, alone in another room.

For her part, it seems to me now, I became something to blame, someone who could be held responsible for what otherwise seemed a meaningless, haphazard cruelty by a God whom we had always been told was loving and caring. I could have done nothing, you may say, to prevent the baby's death, but on the other hand it wouldn't have happened if I hadn't brought her to this barbaric place, with its foul airs and pestilences.

Perhaps if she'd been prepared to give Malaya a chance . . . There were women, after all, I've met plenty of them, who went through what she had gone through. Women who had lived in remote, lonely, malaria-ridden places, who had been tortured by homesickness. Yes, who had lost children too, and who nevertheless had come to love and understand something of it all. Why wouldn't she even try? Was she weak, was she stubborn? Or was she, in fact, strong, refusing to accept the unacceptable?

Or was it, perhaps – as she told me many times, though I would never accept it – that we should never have married? Certainly I was the one who had made all the running in our courtship and marriage, but there was nothing strange in that. In those years anything else would have been unheard of. She had never repelled me, she had never fought against the idea of our marrying and going east. Not really . . .

Eventually I could take it no longer. I wrote to Tommy and Deirdre, who were still in KL. I remember Deirdre's arrival, cool and beautiful in white with a broad-brimmed hat – Tommy had been unable to come down. She had left their little boy with him and their *amah*. The relief was palpable. She would sit all day with Eileen, holding her hand, listening quietly. I was excluded, I did not try to make myself part of it. It was between women. What did they speak of? Inevitably, for Eileen thought of nothing else, the death. Of me? I don't know. She was calmer, but she was still racked with storms of tears, her hostility to me, though quieter, was still sullenly there.

At night, sometimes, while she slept Deirdre and I sat together over a drink, and I talked to her as I had never been able to talk to my own wife. I told her of my feelings, my grief, my guilt at not being able to comfort Eileen. She was the strength I needed.

She gave me no false comfort. 'Look,' she said, 'she's sick, it's not your fault, it's perfectly understandable. Why doesn't she come with Maurice and stay with us in KL? We'll try and get her to the doctor.'

For all her hatred of Jalong, it proved difficult

enough to get Eileen to agree to move. KL, I think she thought, would mean meeting people and she was in no state of mind for that. But in the end she went and, at the prompting of Deirdre, agreed simply to see Simpson, the adored doctor who had delivered Maurice. To that stolid Englishman, I think, she must have poured out her soul more than she ever did to me, or even to Deirdre. Whatever it was that passed between them I never discovered (so many things I never found out) but eventually I was summoned 'for a chat'. Nervous breakdown, exhaustion, need for total rest, a complete change.

Where could she go but home to Ireland? What could I say? Even as I agreed I knew in my heart of hearts that she would never come back to Malaya. No one said as much, of course. I had a year and a half to go before I was due home leave again and the general understanding was that by then she would have recovered and would return to Malaya once more with me.

I saw her off from Singapore a couple of weeks later, her and Maurice. I can see us now, the three of us standing on deck awkwardly as I said my goodbyes, a wan strained-looking young woman, a small boy in shorts and short-sleeved shirt, his shining hair carefully parted and brushed, and myself. There were messages for home, bags to be listed, last-minute checks of money and passports.

I kissed her clumsily on the cheek. Did I imagine she pulled back as I did so? Then I lifted up my little boy, four years old, a quiet child, precursor to a quiet man. Maurice, always due to take second place to his departed sister in his mother's heart and never to really know his father. He grew up to be reserved . . . no, cold. On the increasingly rare occasions when he contacts me we have nothing to say to each other, nor have I anything to say to his remote wife or his well-behaved, patently bored children, my grandchildren. Would we always have been strangers? At least the presence of his mother in Ireland meant he avoided being sent off, still little more than a toddler, to the chilly care of some preparatory school run in the Catholic manner by nuns. If his sister hadn't died that would have been his fate, and he would probably still have grown into the same unknowable man.

I made my way ashore, the gangplanks were pulled up. There were two blasts from the ship's sirens, people waved and threw streamers. How often have I been part of that scene? I could see Eileen holding Maurice up on one of the decks. My son and heir, my little boy. What was it I once heard an old country woman call a baby in Ireland? 'Aren't you,' said she, 'the thief of all the world?' I was losing him as finally, almost, as I had lost my baby daughter the year before. Neither he nor his mother moved, up there on the ship, but as it pulled away all I felt was relief, relief that I could get on with my life without the emotional storms which had shipwrecked it since our tragedy. This feeling was quickly followed by shame at my selfishness and then by a numbing loneliness, a despairing feeling that I was once again alone in a strange land and that it was a loneliness that would not go away.

Chapter Seven

I AM sitting here motionless. The world seems to be rushing by like an express train in a welter of sound that is meaningless. I am looking at a silver tray, a present from Deirdre who once interested herself in craft work in the state of Kelantan. What hands hammered it out and cut the fine, delicate design around the edges? Whoever it was is probably long gone – they're all gone. Who would have thought that I would be the last? I wasn't even the youngest. No more funerals, even, once a regular part of my life.

Mix. Who was it said I should mix more? Maurice's wife, I think. Mix with whom? Old colonials? There aren't any left. I went to the local pub once, one morning. Two or three locals there, the sort that go to pubs in the morning. Bought them a drink, they asked me about the old days. I could see they were laughing at me behind my back.

Thought about suicide. Not really on for me. Still believe enough of what I was taught when young to think it wrong. Scared of death? Used to be.

> Ay, but to die, and go we know not where;
> To lie in cold obstruction and to rot;
> This sensible warm motion to become
> A kneaded clod.

Shakespeare, don't you know. That 'kneaded clod' is frightening. Decided not to dwell on the subject too much.

Young curate calls sometimes. We haven't much to say to each other. He means well. Not much fun calling on old bores like me, I'm sure. Suggested I go to the Old Folk's Club, or whatever it's called, they were having their Christmas party. Not for me. Paper hats, community singing of carols, turkey dinner, local lady bountifuls dispensing condescending smiles and crackers. Not for me, I told him, I'm quite happy the way I am. Always been used to being on my own.

I was alone when Eileen left me, a face in the crowd, a solitary among people. Nothing very unusual in that in colonial Malaya, where single white men were probably in the majority. I had friends but, apart from my *sais*, Kassim, of whom more later, no one with whom I felt any degree of closeness. Tommy and Deirdre had been transferred up-country again, to a remote area of the east coast. It was impossible for me, reared in a tradition of restraint, to share anything but commonplaces with the people I met, to show my feelings. There could be no intimacy, none of that shorthand of word or gesture which exists between those who delight in each other's company, either through long acquaintance or mutual attraction.

I went to the Club, where I played in tennis tournaments and golf matches. I went to dinner parties where I made polite conversation with men and women, good people, many of whom I knew felt sorry for me. The occasional single white woman was to be met, but there could be no question of any more than politenesses between them and me. If I had not been from that solid, conventional Catholic background that I was, perhaps I might have let myself go, flirted, fallen in love, maybe even have divorced and remarried – not greatly approved of, but not unknown even then.

Maybe I might even have gone in search of a wife, taken leave in Singapore or KL, where there were families with daughters of marriageable age, nurses, other single females. Perhaps even met up with one of those tough Australian women who, rumour had it, arrived in Malaya in search of husbands with their wedding cakes packed in their baggage in airtight tins. Perhaps I might even have married, at a ruinous cost to my career, a native – a Chinese, Malay, Indian or one of those exquisitely beautiful Eurasian girls one met in the course of one's rounds.

But what was I thinking about? So far from being divorced, my marriage hadn't even broken up. To all appearances my wife had gone home on sick leave and would eventually be back, cured and ready to take up again the everyday life of a colonial *memsahib*.

I wrote to her, at first frequently. 'My darling . . .', 'My dearest . . .' Remembering our first courtship, I filled my letters with the foolish endearments which young lovers exchange. Even as I wrote them I knew they reeked of banality and emptiness. The shadow which hung over us was too deep for such frivolities, but I could find no real words to express what we both felt. After I posted one such I had a mental picture of her mother, her mouth tightening as she read my words, for she would surely get her hands on it, perusing every line, construing every sentence, searching for clues to my perfidy, my coldness to her daughter, my general lack of satisfaction as a husband.

Eileen, I knew, whatever she would have planned, would have been unable to keep any secrets from her mother and her sister. No matter how she would have hidden behind her illness at first, her hatred of Malaya, of me and of everything connected with the death of our baby would have poured out before long.

But I knew, too, that her chances of sympathy were scant. For her parents, as for the most of their generation, there was only one reply when faced with an unsatisfactory marriage: you've made your bed, you must lie in it. Go back to your husband, make the best of it. Anything, anything would be better than the shame of a broken marriage, what the neighbours would say and the sly jokes behind their backs in the town.

Mercifully, the death of the child was an acceptable excuse for her return home. There she could stay with Maurice until my next leave, a year hence, but after that there was no redress for her. Meanwhile, appearances would be kept up. My letters, or rather the envelopes with their exotic stamps, showing tigers or strangely garbed sultans, would be shown, and tales of my brilliant career, my march towards an inevitable knighthood, would go forth to all who would listen.

'I'm sitting on the stile, Mary . . .' The year passed uneventfully. I was promoted. My Malay improved, it was better than that of most of my colleagues and it opened up to me the world of the *bumiputera*, the native Malays, literally sons of the soil, so-called to distinguish them from all the other races that jostle together on this narrow peninsula. They are a people I came to love, charming, friendly, living a life of harmony with their beautiful land, with the seasons and the elements.

They were and are a race which some might say is plagued by an enormous aristocracy. With nine states and a royal family to each, titles are everywhere. The worst of them become spoiled by not having enough to do, and Europeanized in the worst way, but they were thankfully in a minority. Others led the way to independence and are now the country's rulers. They were and are courteous and likeable people, firm in their Muslim faith, but not to the point of intolerance, something that may not last now that they hold the handles of power.

The Chinese are to Malaya what Northern Protestants like to think of themselves as being to Ireland, shrewder and more hard-working than the majority race and therefore holding a disproportionate share of the country's wealth. The faults of the Malays, if faults they are, are an inclination to indolence and a preference for the quiet life of the *kampongs* over that of the cities. Or such is the popular belief, which may be a very good reason to question it. True or false, it's a situation which, as at home, holds the seeds of inevitable trouble. But this lies far in the future, I hope.

One letter, one only, reached me in all that year from Eileen. I remember the excitement of receiving it, the Irish stamp, her familiar handwriting. My hands trembled as I opened it. I was a fool to have been so excited.

> *Dear Tim, How are you? I am glad to report we are all well here in Ireland. It has been a very bad summer, unfortunately. We went to Ballybunion for a fortnight in July and only got two decent days the whole time we were there. I received your cheque to cover expenses, thank you. Could you let me have something for the winter as we will need new outfits.*

> *Maurice is growing so fast you would
> hardly know him. He will need new shoes
> and a warm overcoat and he has also grown
> out of his suit. Also, he could do with a new
> school bag and, of course, new books when
> the term starts in September. I myself could
> do with some new stuff, too. You know how
> dear everything is these days.*
>
> *I also think I should give something in at
> home. Mam says I needn't but I think it's
> only fair, so if you could see fit to send, say,
> five pounds a month, I would be very grateful.*
>
> *My parents are both well DG. Father has
> bought some new land out on the Limerick
> road, about fifty acres. They send their best
> wishes, as does Josie who says to tell you she is
> praying for you. Maurice is doing well at
> school and sends you his love. Love, Eileen.*

It was cold, remote, the letter of a dutiful child to an unloved parent. I could almost see her mother standing over her, forcing her to write. No mention of our dead baby. No mention of Malaya or even herself, nothing of intimacy. My heart went cold as I read it and my longing for home became tinged with a sickening apprehension.

Just before my leave came up I went up-country to spend a few days with Tommy and Deirdre. They were parents, by now, of two little boys, the elder of whom, a jolly five-year-old, would come into my room in the mornings and bounce on my bed, throwing himself at me like a puppy in a frenzy of good humour that delighted me, while causing me pangs of loneliness for my own son. He's now something to do with the United Nations in Geneva and a father himself. He came to visit me once and spoke with such affection and understanding of his parents that, again, I felt envious, comparing him with my own correctly cold Maurice, who cannot bring himself to talk to me in more than platitudes, and can hardly wait to drive away in his large car when he does visit.

I talked to Tommy about Eileen, but though he was sympathetic and supportive, there was little he could offer me by way of practical advice. Each in our way we were, I suppose, men of our times, taught the value of reticence, uneasy at making our feelings too apparent, afraid to seem weak or vulnerable. Bloody fools! The next generation, I hope, will be less bottled up in themselves.

Or maybe it's just a male thing. Certainly it was easier with Deirdre, but then it always had been. To her I spoke of my loneliness, my fears, my missing wife and child. Once I broke down. Tommy must have been away working or something, maybe I'd had a *pahit* or two over the odds. All I know is that suddenly I was in tears. Tears, me! Not the done thing!

Then her arms were around me and I was sobbing. I clung to her, clung to her. Then I was kissing her. She pushed me away.

'I'm sorry,' I said, 'I'm so sorry.' I felt ashamed of myself, a fool with my blotched wet face.

'It's all right,' she said. 'All right.'

We neither of us mentioned it to Tommy. I don't think he'd have understood.

We had other, less traumatic talks. Her sympathies were with Eileen, for as a mother she could understand the reality of the loss of a child. Again, I felt slightly ashamed at my lack of patience, my failure to provide some degree of consolation for what had happened.

'Give it time, give it time,' said kind, loving Deirdre, and I'm sure she was right, but time was something which I lacked.

Before I left them Tommy and I made an expedition into the jungle. We were still young and fit then and needed to be, for the aboriginal guides who took us up into the densely forested mountains moved with a speed and a sureness that were almost impossible to match. Up we went through the steaming foothills, through tall waving grasses and dense scrub, great patches of wet sweat discolouring our shirts, then into a bamboo thicket as tall as a house and then into the deep jungle.

As we moved through that twilight world I felt, as never before, something I can only describe as mystical. The jungle lives – a truism you may say, but it is more than the sum of its parts, all those millions upon millions of trees, bushes, creepers and God knows what else. It has a life, an entity of its own, from time immemorial, self-perpetuating, all-engulfing, which fills one with awe. It is haunting, over-powering and somewhat frightening.

How easy to lose oneself in this green wilderness and never be seen again. Maybe that's the attraction, for attraction there is, the feeling of a force greater than oneself, greater than man. In much the same way as some men yearn for the sea, others, Europeans, become obsessed with this huge wilderness, vanishing into it for longer and longer spells. And, like the sea, it claims its victims.

All day we wandered through this green twilit ocean, the shade broken only by the occasional flash of brilliant sun penetrating a gap in the canopy above. The heat was stifling, at times one could scarcely breathe. Sweat ran down our faces and into our eyes

111

as we scrambled and plunged over ridges, boulders and fallen trees, tripping over vines and creepers while inch-long thorns clutched at our clothes, or thorny rattan, like barbed wire, entangled itself on our clothes and our skin. Then there would be a sudden drop in temperature, tiny, perhaps, but enough to relieve both body and spirit. It signalled that we were near a river or stream and the bliss of bathing one's face and hands or, better still, sitting under a little waterfall while the clear jungle waters gushed over one's tired boiled body.

I remember following one such stream up towards its source, through a tunnel of greenery that made a roof overhead. We slipped and slid along the narrow banks. Dragon-flies as big as your middle finger, coloured vivid electric blues and greens, hovered motionless like helicopters over the water, while, in the trees above, an unseen band of gibbons crashed through the branches, whooping like crying babies. Two flashes of startling colour signalled the appearance and disappearance of a pair of kingfishers.

Suddenly the light brightened and we were on the banks of a small lake. There, awaiting us, though how anyone knew we were coming I couldn't figure out, were a pair of rafts made of bamboo trunks roughly lashed together. With our guides, we scrambled aboard and, using long bamboos again, we were poled across the brown waters. As we went two huge birds, fish eagles, circled over us uttering harsh cries.

At the other side was a small clearing on which stood a tiny *attap* hut, little more than a platform raised on short stilts. A small man with a blowpipe taller than himself stood waiting for us. As we landed we saw he was not alone. His son, tiny with huge brown eyes, stood beside him looking at us seriously, and lying out on a hammock, stretched between two trees, was his wife. She was naked to the sarong around her waist with jet black curly hair hanging luxuriously down to the ground. It is the height of bad form for any stranger to do other than ignore a *sakai* woman (we called them *sakai* or slaves then, now the less insulting *orang asli* or 'original people' is used). Yet I could not take my eyes off her. She was no beauty, but her languor, her total relaxation and her utter indifference to our presence were, somehow, powerfully erotic. It was as if she had unlocked something in my brain and I found myself aroused in a way I had not been for years.

But, of course, I said nothing and gave, I hope, no sign. Our guides were deep in conversation with her husband. I smiled and said hello to the little boy, but he looked back at me without a flicker of expression on his face. To him I was a creature from another planet, ugly probably, even revolting. We gave the man some small goods, a little tobacco and some salt and passed on our way.

That night, when we made camp, I felt an itchiness around my ankle. Pulling off my boot I saw my sock was covered in blood. I pulled it off. There, disgustingly, was a cluster of leeches, fat with my blood, pulsating, gorging themselves on me like a bunch of living black grapes. Some of them fell to the ground, where they would lie until they had digested their feed and reverted to their matchstick-like shape, ready to move with incredible speed, leap on any other living thing that passed near and clamp their suckers on its skin. I stamped on the ones that had fallen and my blood spurted out from them. The others stuck to me like, well, leeches. The only way to get rid of them was with the lighted end of a cigarette.

Chapter Eight

AND SO, six years after I had first arrived in Malaya, I returned to Ireland for the second time, by way of Singapore, with its hundreds of ships, by Ceylon, that most beautiful of islands, by Bombay where the vultures wheel over the towers on which they expose their dead. Aden then, dusty, fly-blown and unbearably hot, Suez with its over-importunate vendors, the long arrow-straight canal through the desert, Malta with the fleet at anchor, Gibraltar another of Empire's bastions, and rolling up the Bay of Biscay, cold and sea-sick. Docking finally in Liverpool in fog. Tea and hot buttered toast with strawberry jam and the light failing in the early afternoon. A last hop across the Irish sea and I am home.

Home! If my last leave had been something of a triumph, returning from a far exotic land to claim my bride, this was all anti-climax. To begin with, it was winter. The world was sodden. Despite warm underwear and a heavy overcoat my teeth chattered all the time. As we drove south through the drenched land, the small towns of Ireland were a misery of empty streets and weeping walls. Bleak winds drove squalls of rain across the boggy land, the air smelt of turf smoke and animal dung, and over everything there seemed to be an air of poverty and defeat, not least my own.

My father had died the year before, felled by a sudden heart attack as he walked his land alone. He had lain, they reckoned, for three hours, half hidden by a hedge, until one of his farm labourers had found him and, by then, was past all saving. The news came to me in Malaya like a thunderclap. He had been a man around whom the entire life of our family so revolved that it seemed impossible to imagine things without him. Certainly the heart and centre seemed to have gone out of the farm and home which he had so dominated.

My mother was still there, calm and correct but older and, like everything else, diminished. My brother, Ted, had inherited the farm, and he, his wife and small daughters tried to make it seem as always. There were still the animals, the fields, the long, silent meals, the parlour that smelled musty because it was so rarely opened, the rituals of milking and sowing and making hay, of the cows in the cowhouse and the pigs in their sty, of the dairy with its pails of muslin-covered milk and its butter churn. The family still drove to mass in the same trap, pulled by the same pony, and in the evenings still said the rosary, with all the trimmings, for all those on the missions, and especially my brother, Johnny, for so and so who was doing an exam, and such and such who was sick, and for the soul of Father himself and all our multitudinous relations who were, presumably, doing time in Purgatory before being released into eternal beatitude.

But it lacked something, the central figure to whom everything had to be referred ultimately. The stern patriarch, who knelt before the picture of the Sacred Heart that had eyes which followed you around the room, (something that terrified me when I was small). Woe

115

betide you if you were five minutes late for that nightly ritual, or showed the slightest sign of levity, or boredom or impatience as the decades and prayers rolled on sonorously and interminably.

Ted, a nice man with a wife who had a stronger personality than his, lacked *gravitas*. He could sing a good song and was always called on at parties for 'Boolavogue', 'The West's Awake', or some other patriotic ballad, including since I had been away, 'The Boys who bate the Black and Tans were the Boys from the County Cork'. But the awe, and indeed fear, which my father had engendered had gone with him, and I immediately noticed that some of my older nephews and nieces were going missing at rosary time, often on the slimmest excuses. Indeed, the last time I was home, many years on at the funeral of my brother Johnny, only Ted and his wife Mary still kept it up, and in a much truncated form, with the trimmings left out.

And what did they make of the fact that I seemed to be minus a wife? I had, of course, prepared an excuse. Her father was not well, I said, she couldn't leave her mother alone and I would be joining them shortly. They said nothing; in our family personal affairs were only discussed when there was no alternative, feelings never. Inside us we all churned up our guilts, our envies, our prides and our lusts, but they rarely, if ever, escaped, and then only in sudden bursts of anger, of violence even.

I can remember from my youth bad feeling between two of my brothers. Nothing was said for weeks, the customary silence between them became if anything deeper, that was all. Then over some utter triviality, who should have the use of the pony and trap, or some such, they fell on each other and fought with a fierceness and savagery that if weapons had been to hand could have ended in death.

Father had come upon them and beaten them apart with a riding crop, leaving a red weal across the face of one. For an instant his son had frozen, hate in his eyes, as if to turn on my father as well. Then fear, awe, sense, something had stopped him and he ran out of the room. It was Mick, who was killed in the war. The matter was never referred to again, by any of them, and the quarrel seemed to end with the fight. What was it all about in the first place? For the life of me I can't remember, if I ever knew.

Anyway, no one was going to draw me out on the subject of my marriage. The closest was my mother. I see her now, sewing, beside a window.

'And how is Eileen?'

'Well,' I answer.

There is a long pause.

'She's recovered from the nerves?'

'Yes, she seems to be fine again.' I don't tell her that the only news I have had of my wife's health has been in a letter from her sister, who puts her cure down to the power of prayer, and why not?

'To lose a child is hard.' She has had fourteen, two dead in infancy and how many miscarriages? Two down and twelve to go. Yes, to lose a child is hard.

'She'll be going back with you, then?'

'Yes.' She knows, I know she knows, but do I know myself? Or, knowing, can I tell myself? 'Yes, yes she'll be going back with me. I'm going to stay with her parents. Her father is getting better. Yes, we'll be returning to Malaya as soon as my leave is up.'

I can't even talk to my own mother. To say . . . what? That, in my heart, I know my marriage has ended, to ask her what can I do, how can I save it? How can I say it when no one else has done so?

What would she say, anyway? The same as Eileen's family. You've made your bed, you must lie in it. Had she not seen two of her own daughters have their marriages made for them. Indeed, her own marriage had been so arranged and I had never thought of it as anything but a success. Maybe it would have been better for me, too. Maybe I would have had someone chosen for me who would have fought in the valleys of life and rejoiced on its pinnacles, who would have seen my weakness and coped with it and, if not, I could have had someone else other than myself to blame for what went wrong. But I had made my own choice, there had been no coercion, no question of dowries or other arrangements. And so had Eileen. Therefore we must stick by each other, and why not when so many others were in far worse situations than ours?

I drove across the saturated land to Eileen's home and knocked on the solid door of her solid family house on the outskirts of town. My heart was in my mouth. How was I to approach this? What would we say? What would we do? Would we be sharing a bedroom?

The door opened. It was the maid. Behind her in the hall I could see Eileen, with little Maurice holding her hand. I stepped forward and at that moment a wheezing, snarling ball of hair shot at me. It was Trap, her mother's malevolent old cocker spaniel, over-weight, bad-tempered and given to emitting farts of an unparalleled foulness, which in that ultra-polite family circle nobody ever mentioned – just moved away discreetly, turning their heads from the effluence or pretending to blow their noses.

Usually Trap contented himself with rumbling threats against my person, but on this occasion he went straight to work, sinking his teeth into my ankle. Perhaps he was just showing an honesty which nobody else was. The maid, her mistress being absent, dispatched the dog with a well-placed kick, while I hopped around. The pain was agonizing but the ice was broken.

They all gathered round me. There were no kisses, no awkward greetings. Iodine was produced and a bandage, the dog was banished to exterior darkness. Her mother came in, her father was summoned from the shop down the town. Tea was sent for. Eventually I was settled in a chair.

I looked over at Eileen. I had thought of her so much since she had left, had missed her, had run over in my mind what had happened, trying to make sense of it, trying to see who was to blame, if anyone was. What did she now think? Did she still hold me responsible? Was there any warmth for me left in her heart? She looked well, better certainly than the strained, fragile woman I had seen off on the boat. She smiled, she talked, but I knew, in the way one always knows about someone with whom intimacy has been shared, that things were not right, that I was not welcome.

The small boy, my son, stood in front of me impassively.

'Well, Maurice . . .' I held out my arms to him.

'How do you do, Mr O'Hagan,' he said, putting out his hand.

Laughter all round. Maurice! This is your daddy. Give your daddy a kiss. No, no, it's been so long. He's got so big. Isn't he the image of your father? Everyone thinks he's the image of your father. We were very sorry to hear. And how is your mother? And your brother

Father John, have you heard from him lately? And his Grace the Bishop?

The commonplaces continue. Her father arrives, breathing heavily from the exertion of hurrying up from his place of business. He has angina. He is effusive. 'How are you, Tim, boy? You're looking powerful.' Immediately he is talking about money. Things were never worse. The farmers are ruined. The amount of bad debt is scandalous. The clergy should preach about it and not be on eternally about dances and jazz music and courting. His wife's mouth purses in disapproval and he hastily back-tracks. Not that that isn't a disgrace too. He could tell me stories. There's a fella in this very town and he has two women—

'More tea?' His wife moves in hastily to stem the tide of hideous scandal, her eyes ablaze at the crudity of her mate.

I look over at Eileen. She avoids my gaze. She has risen at her father's entrance and he has taken the armchair in which she was sitting. She is forced to place herself beside me on the sofa. I put her hand in mine. It sits there, passive.

Then it's time to bring my bags upstairs, while Eileen hovers in the background. We are in a room together. Her room. It is a woman's room, a room that hasn't seen a man. A big double bed, though, a dressing table with silver-backed brushes and comb, a big bottle of eau-de-Cologne which has perfumed the air. A wardrobe full of her clothes, she always dressed well. And, in the corner, Maurice's cot.

Isn't he getting a bit big for that? Shouldn't he be in a room of his own? Oh, she has him ruined, her mother tells me later with a laugh, for she herself adores the little boy just as much, and spoils him just as fondly.

Eileen, who had always seemed to me to be rather remote from the child in Malaya, has now transferred to him all her love, all her hopes for the future and smothers him in affection and care.

I now ask myself, what did she really feel for him, did she really love him so much? Was it a way of getting at me, of trying to ensure she would not have to return to that faraway, hated land. If her love for him was as warm as she pretended, why did he grow into such a cold fish? Or was it that her love came, even then, too late, transferred to him only after the death of his really-loved baby sister? But these are matters for priests or psychologists, and probably admit no secure answers.

That night we shared our room with the sleeping child in the cot. We undressed like strangers forced to share a hotel room, or people on a public beach, hiding our bodies in wrappings as we disrobed. Eileen knelt by the bed in her dressing gown and said lengthy silent prayers, and I, who had got out of the habit since she left, did the same, slightly ashamed of my hypocrisy. We slid between the sheets and she turned out the light. I lay silent in the cold envelope, then put out a tentative hand towards hers. She turned her back.

'Good night,' she said, and I knew my fears were well founded.

When was it that we finally had things out? It's so long ago. I seem to remember a long country walk, through thin winter hedges. Sullen rivers, half light, cattle staring over ditches.

'You know,' I said, 'that Maurice will have to stay behind when we go back.'

'What?' she asked, as if it came to her as an unwelcome surprise, though she must have known full well that if she went back with me the little boy would have to remain with his grandmother.

'What choice have we?' I said.

'No! No, no!' The storm broke all the more furiously after the silence. All the old hatred of the East and, because of it, of me poured out as it had after the death of our baby.

'I'm not going back, I'm not leaving Maurice. I hate it out there. I never wanted to go there, you dragged me out, you know I always hated it.'

'I did not drag you out. You went of your own free will. You never said you didn't want to go.'

'My baby would still be alive if we'd stayed at home.'

'She was my baby, too.'

'We should never have married.'

Her outbreak provoked a similar one in me, of intense anger.

'Have you no loyalty? Did you ever make the slightest attempt to understand me or my life? You never even tried to come to terms with it. All you can think of is your little parochial world.'

'We should never have married.' The old refrain.

'I never forced you to marry. Did you ever by any word or deed so much as hint you didn't want to go through with it?'

'Please don't shout. Do you want people to hear you?' We were out in the middle of the country in the rain. There wasn't a soul in sight. Silence returned.

Oh, those long evenings in that underlit parlour, with the antimacassars on the chairs, the smouldering turf fire. Her father discussing the price of cattle endlessly, her mother disapproving of him, Eileen and I sitting silently, the dog passing wind.

But there was a crisis and at last her family had to take notice of it. She had taken her courage in her hands and told them the appalling news. It was a catastrophe, the end of their dreams for her, a violent storm in the calm waters of their existence. They were torn between their loyalty to their daughter – if something was wrong it must be my fault – and their fear and hatred of the scandal that a broken marriage would bring. Of course, the fear of scandal won. Also, when they looked into it, it all seemed inexplicable. I wasn't beating her, or drinking, or having affairs with other women, so what was wrong?

There was a visit to the convent of her sister Josie, the nun. I remember a highly polished parlour with pictures of the Pope and the foundress of the Order. Then the usual huge feed of meat and potatoes, at the end of which the then Reverend Mother, who had sat with us but not eaten, withdrew. Josie got the proceedings going with a not-so-short homily on the meaning of the sacrament of marriage – if she had been a man she would have made a sonorous preacher – followed by the not very profound statement that a wife should stick by her husband, the reverse of which was also true.

Eileen tried to defend her position. She spoke, haltingly, of her hatred of Malaya, its people, its climate and of the death of her baby girl. She spoke of the horror of leaving little Maurice behind and not seeing him for three years. She made her case poorly, with the tentativeness of someone who is used to having their side of the argument over-ridden. She did not mention her feelings for me.

Josie took it all in her stride.

'I've talked to Mama,' she said. 'She'll be only too

123

pleased, delighted in fact, to care for Maurice. There'll be no need for him to go away to school, though, God knows, the sisters there would care well for him.'

'I hate it out there. It's lonely. I don't want to go back,' said Eileen.

'Given time,' said Josie, 'I've no doubt you'll come to like it better.'

'It'd be three years before I saw Maurice again.'

'Sure, three years is nothing. Give it another chance, you owe it to Tim here. We know it's been hard for you, but God is good. I'm sure ye'll have more children.'

She mentioned the comfort of prayer, and promised to storm heaven on our behalf during a forthcoming retreat, making particular representations to St Therese, the Little Flower, Patroness of the Foreign Missions. She asked about the position of the Catholic Church in both the Federated Malay States and the Straits Settlements. I, who had been sitting dumb through all this, assured her that there were no shortage of priests and churches out there, and, for her, that settled it.

Even then I felt sorry for Eileen. Father, mother and sister, all were united against her. She had a friend, Maisie, living in Limerick who had been at school with her and was, I think, her only ally in the world. It was a joke at first, Maisie and I never hit it off. She was a thin woman with prominent teeth, who smoked incessantly and always, in my memory, seemed to be wearing a hat. She was famed as a dedicated and virulent gossip and didn't seem to have a good word to say about anybody. I think she resented me for taking away Eileen.

She had never married herself, though years before she had had a 'romance', as she called it, with a young teacher, who had broken it off, unable, I'm sure, to

124

cope with her acid tongue. He was, as she never tired of telling us, 'a bit of a mammy's boy', hinting that his sexual preferences were not what they should be. Her friendship with Eileen was renewed when she returned after the baby's death. She would pour bile about everything and everyone into her friend's ear and I'm sure much of what my wife subsequently said to me was inspired from that direction.

But as an ally she carried no weight. Slowly, remorselessly the family ground down Eileen's objections. I could see the terrified look in her eyes, at night I could hear her cry. I should have said, all right, let's give it some more time. Come out later. Maybe if I'd done that she might have come round eventually, but I did nothing, save make a few clumsy attempts at comforting her, which she rejected out of hand. It was settled. I had a month left of my leave and then we would return together, leaving our five-year-old behind. Then fate took a hand, or maybe her prayers were answered.

He was called William O'Brien, a common enough name in that part of the world, but one which I have cause to remember. He was a strong farmer, notable only for the fact that he owned a Ford car and was seventy-two years of age. In those days cars were few and far between, but I was told that he had inherited money from a brother in America, a bachelor like himself. It was his practice to drive the twisting roads of the area at a steady sixty miles an hour, never deviating from the middle of the road, and that is what he was doing at twilight one evening when Eileen's mother was taking her nightly constitutional with her dog.

I remember the evidence at the inquest. Coming round a corner he found himself confronted with the

noisome Trap waddling along in mid-stream. Normally
. . .ld have proceeded straight over the animal but
something, maybe the half bottle of whiskey and the
box of chocolates he had just consumed as was his wont
in the local pub-grocery, had temporarily sharpened his
reflexes. Anyway, he swerved sharply and went straight
into Trap's mistress, who was walking behind on the
edge of the road. The impact knocked her out and
threw her into the ditch. She died some hours later,
never having regained consciousness, fortunately for
her killer who would undoubtedly otherwise have
received a tongue-lashing that might have done for him
also.

Such grief! Such relief! Eileen had found herself a
new role. Before her mother was buried she had become
the new head of the household, the guardian of her
grief-stricken father, and him with a bad heart.

She made all the funeral arrangements, saw the
house was spick and span, cooked huge amounts of
food and welcomed all the outlying members of the
family who attended. She seemed, almost overnight, to
grow in authority, to have stepped into her dead
mother's shoes.

At the funeral I played a very small role. The
assorted uncles, aunts and cousins who had gathered
spoke to me politely. Many of them had been at our
wedding and, of course, neither by word nor hint did
they know anything of the problem of our marriage.

Stephen turned up, the black sheep brother, who
had been absent when we married – had he been
invited? He looked old beyond his years and slightly
shabby. He showed few signs of grief. His history meant
that whatever affection had existed between himself
and his mother was long gone, and Eileen had told me

that her father used to beat him long and mercilessly when he was a boy – hardly conducive to a loving relationship. There was no sign of his wife, who was English and, it was suspected, socially inferior.

He viewed the proceedings with a sardonic eye, making scurrilous remarks to me about his various relatives out of the corner of his mouth.

'See that fella?' – about an uncle – 'The meanest man in the County Limerick, *including* my father.' Or about an eminently respectable-looking matron. 'One of them nymphomaniacs. Had more rides than a Grand National winner. He, he, he.' He had a high-pitched snigger.

His sisters treated him with ill-disguised contempt.

'Look at that fool of a man,' said Josie to me, as he helped himself to a third too-large whiskey after the funeral.

Before he went back to wherever he lived in England he borrowed money from me. I gave him a tenner.

'It'll be with you by the end of the week,' he said, unblushingly. I thought him pathetic.

But the best, for Eileen, was to come after the funeral guests had departed. She would have to stay, she said, to care for her father, a sick man now alone in the world with nobody to keep house for him. She would go East later – an unspecified later that could mean a month, a year, or even longer. Her father and sister, thrown by the sudden and totally unexpected death of the domineering mother and probably glad enough to have her support, agreed it might be for the best.

And me? I was worn down by constant arguments, angry with Eileen, uncertain of my feelings for her. My only wish, at that stage, was to get away from this wet, dismal, unhappy country and return to the sunshine and colour of the East. In my heart I must have known that the break this time would be final, but I didn't want to look beyond the immediate future.

'Sure, you won't feel the time till she's back out with you,' said Josie, and I hope she admitted to what she surely knew was a lie next time she went to confession.

Her father grasped my hands in both of his large red ones, whiskey tears in his eyes, and thanked me for the consideration I was showing to an old man. I think he saw a bright future for himself, in which there would be no one to sneer at his lack of manners, no one to disparage his dress, or his speech, or to deny him the evenings of drinking with his cronies which he craved but was hardly ever allowed.

In this he was mistaken, for his daughter ruled him with a fist as iron-clad as ever his wife's had been. He remained frustrated and looked down upon until the day he dropped dead during twelve o'clock mass in the local church, 'a lovely death', according to Josie.

And so I left that wet unhappy small town, and returned to Malaya alone.

Chapter Nine

I SIT here in a cane chair, looking out at the garden. Brown and black birds are pecking at a flower bed, the sun has gone out and the grey skies of Ireland mute every colour. No sign of help, of doctor or ambulance or any of those body mechanics who will shortly be prodding me and questioning me and needling me. Here am I, all alone, waiting . . . So what has changed? This is what I've been doing for these last ten years, waiting, waiting for the end. Locked into myself, though at least I could communicate then, in a limited fashion. Communicate I'd like a cup of tea please, or ask the milkman to leave a bottle less, or nice day, isn't it? But feelings, intimacies, I lost that facility years ago.

It's strange how death intervened twice to separate myself and my wife, the first time to send her home from Malaya, the second to save her from returning. I acted correctly, of course, making her an allowance which, I was to discover later, she did not need.

With its foul stench of rotten eggs and worse, its bright yellow unhealthy-looking pulp and its initial decaying oniony garlicy taste, few Europeans can face the durian at first. But with time and persistence all that can change. The strange flavour becomes piquant and reveals an amazing delicacy, quite hidden to begin with, and even the vile odour becomes somehow fragrant, rich.

Back in Malaya I felt better. I was glad to return from the cold sopping land of my birth. It was ten years since I had first come East and the realization came to me that I now belonged here more than in Ireland. A false feeling really, I suppose, for as a European it could never really be my country. Still, though I no longer had a family there, there was still a life to be led, a life that I loved. I forced myself to mix more socially, played bridge, played tennis, even played rugby despite the fact that, now in my thirties, I was getting a bit old for it in the tropical heat.

I drank heavily, too, copious *stegahs* and *pahits* in a way I had never done before, but which in that bibulous colonial world seemed not excessive at all. It is a habit which has stayed with me to this day, when I often disguise my loneliness to myself by going to bed drunk, or even falling asleep here on the sofa, crumpled and old. When I look in the bathroom mirror next morning I disgust myself.

Most of all though, I threw myself into my work and the country. Malaya, as I have written, is a land of many races, the two main ones, the Malays and Chinese, being almost of similar numbers. In the Civil Service you were assigned to work mainly with one or the other and I was on the Malay side.

Then I was moved to the more rural east coast. The more career-minded, who preferred the cities of the densely populated west called it 'lotus eating', though I didn't mind. Certainly there was a dream-like quality about it, in retrospect anyway, but I never found it dull.

Islam ruled the mainly Malay population and the towns were full of mosques and loud with the cries of the muezzins calling the faithful to prayer. Religious tenets were enforced with a severity that would have gladdened the heart of many an Irish parish priest if the same could have been done for Catholicism. There were fines for Muslims not attending the mosque on Friday, and during Ramadan, the month of fasting, police searched for sinners who were disobeying the rule of no eating or drinking between sunrise and sunset, and dragged them off to jail.

There was a second tier to the MCS, made up of educated English-speaking Malays. Members of the same clubs (the racism of the more populous areas hadn't penetrated here), they mixed with us on friendly terms, and we invited each other to our homes, and played games together. They were easy-going and excellent company, not afraid to talk to us as equals, many of them fathers of the future rulers of their country. Did they, in the privacy of their houses, when we had departed, speak of ancient wrongs and dream of a day when the white man had departed? Possibly, later, but before the war freedom to them meant only a future time when Islam would dominate the avaricious Chinese.

When I got to know more about its history, I came to realize that their country had been first colonized by a familiar mixture of thuggery and double dealing. Broken treaties, the exploitation of local wars and rivalries, the planting of whole areas with foreign settlers, these were familiar tactics to any Irishman. Fortunes had been made by greedy merchants, innocent people had been thrown off their land so that it could be used for new crops.

Yet, apart from the largely Chinese Communist Party, there was no great movement for independence here, as there had always been in Ireland. Why? Were they simply too far away from the nationalist and revolutionary movements that had convulsed the world, East and West, to have reached them at that time? Was it the famed Malay indolence, an attribute which didn't extend to the common people, who toiled mightily in their paddy fields or fishing boats? Was it their Muslim faith, their fear of the wealthier and more astute Chinese, the relative ease of obtaining the necessities of life, their feeling that resistance to the almighty British raj was pointless, or was it a combination of all these? For whatever the reason, they seemed content with their lot. Happy the country without politics!

I like to think that we, the *orang putih*, the white people, and our rule may have had something to do with it. Having got what we wanted, we introduced fair and honest government, and in that hotch-potch of races it was probably the best way to run things ... But I am using exactly the same arguments as the Irish unionists.

The months passed by and turned, with what seemed astonishing speed, into years. Almost as soon as I had settled in, yet another period of home leave loomed ahead. Sometimes I would fool myself that this time, somehow, things would be better, that Eileen would be reconciled to me and that she would return to Malaya with me. In my heart of hearts, of course, I knew otherwise. But even my natural pessimism has its limits and the dream provided me with occasional, if illusory, hope.

A letter from her dashed all this. It left me in no doubt that there would be no welcome waiting for me from her. At the end of the usual banalities about Maurice, her family and even the weather, she wrote (and I could imagine the difficulty it would cause her to say it) that, when I came home, 'it might, in the circumstances, be better if we did not see each other'.

My reaction was, first and foremost, anger. What had I done to deserve this? How could she be so cold, so unfeeling, so, well, so damn unfair? Perhaps I should have let my temper cool off, have given myself time to think, but in a blaze of fury I cancelled my passage home and decided to spend my leave travelling in other eastern countries. If there had been someone in whom I could confide I might have been persuaded to change my mind, but there was nobody with whom I felt like talking about it except Tommy and Deirdre and they were far away at the other end of the country.

I visited Shanghai, that cosmopolitan Chinese city, now changed for ever; I visited Siam with all its beauties; I took passage on a small ship that ran along the Borneo coast, past islands that were like jewels in seas that seemed to change colour from dark blue to shining emerald green. Sea snakes undulated in the water, porpoises gave us friendly escorts as we sailed. At night the water shone with phosphorescence and sometimes we could even make out the banks of rivers by the glow of millions of fireflies along them. In these distant seas pirates still operated and our crew members were armed, but thankfully we encountered none on my trip. In the little ports at which we called we were always given a warm welcome by what few Europeans there were there. Life could be lonely and dreary enough for them and the visit of the boat almost their only diversion, with its supplies of things like bread and fresh meat and a chance to dine aboard with the officers.

After that I went to stay with friends in Sarawak, a country the size of England that was ruled by the Brookes, the celebrated dynasty of white rajas. There I visited the long houses of the *dayak* peoples and saw mummified heads hanging from the rafters, though the custom of head-hunting was by then coming to an end. There we forced ourselves to eat a revolting meal of rice and the toughest fowl I have ever encountered, followed by a session in which the leading women of the place sang odes of welcome to us and we drank large quantities of a fiery rice wine. There was music after that and the men intoned lengthy epic poems, incomprehensible to me, about heroic deeds of the past. Hospitality in ancient Ireland must have been very similar.

The months passed agreeably and I found travelling stimulating and pleasant in that world where the white man was still almost always greeted with deference and the best of everything. But it would mean that eight years would elapse between the time I had last gone back to Ireland and the time I would be back there again. Too long. It would weaken my ties with my country in a way which could never be repaired.

Back in Malaya things were changing for those of us in the MCS. The civil servant, once a master of all trades and an absolute ruler in his own little district, was now faced with increasing specialization. Bit by bit, we were being hived off into health, legal or education departments, run by an increasingly centralized bureaucracy. I knew when I went back to my administration job on the east coast that it would not be for long.

Kassim, my *sais*, or driver, had come to me in my first year in Malaya. He had the graceful, trim figure of the typical Malay, with a nut-brown face on which there sat a perpetual grin. He was one of the half dozen or so servants that even the most modestly paid Europeans could afford, but unlike the others, who came and went with my various postings, he was to stay with me all my time there. Between us there grew a friendship closer than any other I made among the Malays.

He never learned more than a few words of English: 'Damfull', addressed out the window of the car at passing traffic – Malaya contains one of the world's heaviest concentrations of bad drivers – or 'bloddy bastard', for anybody else who displeased him.

He had a wife and children but viewed my marital misfortunes with a tolerant shrug of his shoulders. Yet the fact that there was no replacement for my wife seemed odd to him, celibacy being virtually unknown in Islam. For him divorce would have been relatively easy, had he ever wanted it, or he could just have taken a second wife. It was a system which I often thought far superior to the Jansenist Catholicism of my native land, with its sex-obsessed, sex-hating clergy who blighted the private lives of so many people in the name of a just God.

Of course, it was a different matter for women, who had even fewer rights than their Irish sisters. But the Muslim faith in Malaya at that time was more tolerant in practice than in law. Women did not wear the veil and moved freely in public. Like their equivalents in Ireland, too, Malay womenfolk were very often the strong, outspoken and undisputed bosses of their own families.

Kassim drove me around the limited roads of the state in a gleaming black Vauxhall that was the joy of his life, and which he polished incessantly. As we went on our rounds we chatted about everything under the sun – well, not quite everything, for we never seemed to mention the *mem* who had gone away with my child and never returned.

Once he said to me that I should take another wife,

a Malay, and that the most beautiful and desirable of women could be mine, if I would convert to Islam. Maybe he had seen my eyes turning to some beauty we had passed on the road. I paused for an instant – it was not unknown after all for such things to happen – but then shook my head. He, in his manner, roared with laughter and the moment passed.

Imagine it, in that conservative world before the war, if I had taken up such an offer. The scandal, the comings and goings: 'Heard about O'Hagan? He's gone native'; the veiled threats to my career; the unwanted allies among the more extreme of my new fellow-religionists; the uncomprehending horror among my family at home, my brother Johnny, perhaps because of his experiences among the Chinese, one of the most unbending of Catholics. Such sacrifices, such cutting oneself off from everything one belonged to, and for what? At best, sexual gratification, a family life – but very different from one's own upbringing – half-caste children who would hover between two worlds, the breaking of all contacts with home. No, it would take more courage, more disillusion with my life than I then had, most of all, probably, more powerful emotion, a love or anyway a sexual passion stronger than I felt for anybody at that time. But I was still a young man, a normal man, and no natural celibate – if there is such a thing.

She was older than me, fast, hard, outspoken, and married. Her husband, George Rummage, was an expert on aborigines, one of those men of whom I have written who became obsessed with the deep jungle and its inhabitants. When you visited their house you were apt to find small men wearing only loin cloths squatting on the floor, smoking rank tobacco or chewing betelnuts, pausing only to eject gobbets of red-stained spittle from their mouths. He and they talked about God-only-knows-what in a strange grunting tongue that was quite incomprehensible to most people, and they would vanish and reappear, apparently without motive.

That was when he was at home. For much of the time, however, he was absent on long treks through that amazing wilderness. He was a civil and not very exceptional man in every other way, but there was something about him, a faraway look in his eyes, and abstraction in his conversation, so that you felt some-times as if there was someone else in the room whom you could not see. He had found ancient stones in the jungle, allegedly traces of a lost city, a civilization that had vanished long before the first Europeans had pene-trated that country. To most people they were, well, stones and no more, but he spoke of them with a passion that nothing else seemed to ignite in him.

Certainly not his wife. She had been, I would imagine, a good-looking, even beautiful girl, but the first bloom was well off her by now – the climate of the East can be cruelly ageing to some European women. What did she look like? I remember people, what they said, how they behaved, but their faces seem blurred. Brown skin that the sun had wrinkled, permed hair. Red, yes red. No, not her hair, her mouth, her nails. She looked ... yes, tough is the word for it, I suppose.

Yet this toughness was stimulating to me. It was the sexual attraction of an older woman to a young man, the promise of experience, of breaking the rules, of doing things which were only fantasies to me. I suppose I used to glance at her covertly in the Club, maybe when we played bridge or tennis. Anyway she would have known that I was attracted; people like that can see the signs.

One evening I arrived at the Club earlier than usual. It was empty except for her, and four women playing one of those never-ending games of bridge which seemed to go on round the clock there. She was sitting alone at a table, a drink in front of her, reading a novel. The instant she looked up I could see her interest in me.

I ordered a couple of drinks for us and asked her how George was.

'George?' she said, with a too-loud laugh that momentarily caused the card players to turn their heads. 'George is ... terrific!' She raised her glass. 'Here's to good old George!' And she downed it in one. The bridge ladies talked a little louder among themselves.

'Out in the *ulu*, is he?' I asked.

'Where else? Don't you know he's *always* out in the bloody *ulu*. Every time he goes out into that jungle he's gone longer.'

'Well, it gets to people,' I said, rather fatuously.

'Well, it's certainly got to good old George. I haven't seen him for a month.'

'There's something about the jungle, you know, Mrs Rummage.' God, I must have sounded so pompous.

'Yes, there's a lot of trees in it.' Again she laughed loudly. 'And, for God's sake, stop calling me Mrs Rummage. Call me Primrose, everyone else does. Boy!' She waved her glass in the direction from which the drinks came. 'What a damned silly name, Primrose Rummage! Some people shorten it to Prim, but that doesn't really suit me, does it? As I'm bloody sure you've been told.'

I realized she must have been drinking for some

time. 'I don't pay too much attention to gossip,' I said.

'Don't you? Just as well in your case, old boy.'

It was at that point I should have made my excuses and left. But, of course, I didn't want to. 'What does that mean?' I said stiffly.

'How long has that wife of yours been gone now?'

'I fail to see that that is any business of—'

Again the laugh: 'Oh, come on, Tim, don't get all stuffed shirt with me, I don't mean any harm, truly. What do you do with yourself in your spare time?'

'What does anyone do? Golf, tennis, swim, come down here to the Club.'

She looked at me, and for the first time I saw something else there.

'Gets to you, doesn't it?' she said.

'Sometimes, yes.'

'Ever hear from her?'

'Yes, a couple of times.'

'Think she'll come back?'

There! The question nobody ever asked me.

I answered haltingly. 'She ... she says she will, when she's had a bit more time at home ...'

Her hand brushed lightly against mine. How can I remember that, when I can remember so little else? It was electric.

'That's hard for you.' She was looking straight into my eyes. I was trying to avoid her gaze and failing.

'Harder for her,' I said. 'Losing our little girl, and anyway she never liked Malaya.'

'I know how she felt. At least she had a husband who was there sometimes, and not trekking round the jungle with little men with blowpipes.'

'Did you ever think of going home yourself?' Then: 'Sorry, none of my affair.'

'Of course I have. I've thought about it lots of times. But what would I go back to? Does your wife have a family back there?'

'My wife has a family like a warren has rabbits.'

She laughed again. The bridge players seemed to have become totally immersed in their game.

'Then she's lucky,' said Primrose.

'Lucky? I suppose so.'

'Yes, I haven't a soul, apart from a cousin I hardly know. Imagine me back home in some freezing cottage in Bournemouth or Torquay. What would I do? Stoke the fire, go to the lending library, turn to the gin bottle . . . speaking of which . . .'

'Oh, sorry. Boy!' He came and I ordered the same again.

'Ha!' said Primrose triumphantly.

'What's wrong?'

'I just caught a look from that old biddy Joan Brown. You and I, my boy, are going to be the talk of the bridge tables.'

'Well, bully for the bridge tables.'

'And bully for you, Tim!' She smiled and again looked straight into my eyes.

'How long before you expect George back?'

She paused. 'Listen, Tim, you don't want to get involved with me. A nice clean-living young chap with a career in front of him. I'm the Fallen Woman around here, you know, the planters' friend, the toast of the officers' mess – so they'll tell you.'

'I only asked when George would be back.'

'George will never be back. Oh, he'll turn up one of these days, but he'll be dreaming of the jungle and the rivers and his bloody *sakai*. He's not really there any more. He's retreated into himself, into some half-native, I-don't-know-what. Whatever it is, I'm shut out of it. My own fault, I expect. God knows, I've hardly been the perfect wife.'

Her eyes brimmed. She lit a cigarette and drew on it fiercely.

'You know,' I told her, 'I was always a bit scared of you.'

She barked a laugh. 'Of me? Oh, the scarlet woman thing!'

'You always seemed—'

'I know – loud.'

'No.'

'Yes. Loud and full of gin, and easy – a woman of easy virtue, isn't that what they call it?'

That's what they called it all right.

'You're not really like that at all,' I said.

She laughed. 'Don't be so sure. You're getting me . . . I'll rephrase that . . . you find me on one of my better evenings. I can be a loud, very coarse, very unattractive bitch, if you'll pardon the expression.'

'No. Underneath, I mean. Underneath you're different.'

She was amused, I could see, but pleased, and as for me I didn't care what she was or was not by now.

'How sweet of you to say so, Tim,' she said, 'but I really am like that.'

'No. I refuse to believe it.'

'You know who my *friends* are? Bone stupid army officers who think because they're away from home they can cheat on their wives. Planters whose idea of intellectual exercise is to look at the cricket scores. Travelling salesmen and sea captains and clerks who only want to quieten the itch in their pants, or to do something they can boast about. "Oh yes, a white woman. I had a white woman—" '

'Stop!' I didn't want to hear this. She grinned at me, a death's head grin.

'Why do you do it?' I asked her. I could hear myself, sounding like some preacher about to launch into a hell-fire sermon: Abandon your wicked ways, my child, or you will be cast into eternal flames, reserved for the devil and his angels. 'Why do you do it?'

'Because, my friend,' she said, 'I'm in the business of consolation. I'm consoling myself for my rotten life. And every time I console myself I need more consolation.'

'I could do with some consolation myself,' I said.

'Then have another *pahit* . . .'

That night, after dark, I drove to her bungalow. She was waiting on the verandah. There were no servants to be seen. She was wearing a light dressing gown of silky stuff, no more. Her kiss was . . . voracious, she pressed her body tightly against mine. She hooked her fingers over the top of my belt and led me to her bedroom, without a word.

For me this was something new, something alarming. Sex, in my world and my time, was not something you talked about. When it happened, it happened almost without premeditation. It was something that was granted to you by a woman, never sought. It was a gift she gave you, that was the unspoken pact, and even if she too received pleasure from it that pleasure was largely hidden, to be deduced from moans, or sighs or kisses, not spoken of, not . . . rejoiced in openly.

At least, that had been my experience, a pitifully limited one, I grant you. The world in which I was raised warped our sexuality; how could it do otherwise?

These are beliefs I have never managed to shake off, despite all my experiences in life – a feeling that in the end all that awaits me is damnation. Nowadays they emphasize the merciful, loving side of things more. They're making a mistake. Damnation is much more effective.

Primrose lay back on the bed, her marriage bed. For a moment fear, inhibition, those things I had been so well taught, knocked at my door. But the promise was too great. I was in the hands of an expert. Every movement was a joy. I was amazed, I was proud of myself.

Afterwards we drank gin on her verandah, served by a house boy who materialized with the drinks without being summoned. I suppose it was almost a routine for him, but I was too bemused, too overcome to notice the fact.

After that I visited her twice, three times a week. In the Clubhouse we barely acknowledged each other's existence, but of course they knew, everybody knew. But I didn't care. I didn't even care that one night, when I went to visit her, I found that her husband had returned.

He hardly seemed to notice. I told some mumbled lie about returning a book. He merely smiled, in his usual abstracted fashion. I don't think there was even irony in that smile, as there was in Prim's. He offered me a drink, which I gulped down, acutely conscious of my burning cheeks, then made a lame excuse about having to be off and vanished into the night. He was back into the jungle in no time and the relationship continued.

Later I asked her: 'Does he know?'

'Know what?'

'About us.'

'I daresay.'

'Doesn't he mind?'

'Look, darling, don't be a bore,' she said. 'Get me another drink.'

Another letter, no not a letter, more of a note, from Eileen. She was busy, her father had not been well. The family businesses were falling behind and would need reorganization. She was thinking of selling off some of the land they owned. It was necessary to make sure that every penny was to hand. My cheque had been late last month, could I make certain this did not happen again?

That was about the size of it, no hint again of anything personal, but this time I did not expect it. Involved in my love affair, all I can remember is feeling faintly amused, faintly worried at the idea of Eileen taking the financial reins of her family, as she seemed to be doing.

I nurtured mad ideas of divorce, of throwing up everything and taking off somewhere with Prim. Something stopped me from ever broaching the subject for a long time, but one night, as we lay in her bed, I did mention it. Her reaction startled me – anger, derision. I was sent packing.

Thereafter everything seemed to go wrong. Our love-making continued, as fierce and as consuming as ever, but there were endless sulks, silences and insults. She would fall into thunderously black moods for no reason at all, when she acted as if I wasn't there, or she would scream abuse at me in barrack-room language. 'You drip. You fucking excuse for a man.'

My incompetence as a lover was a constant topic – 'pathetic' was a favourite account of my prowess. My failure to love her. Her lack of love for me. My failure to let the world know that I loved her. My indiscretion so that everybody knew we were lovers. It hardly mattered what she said. The abuse was all. Her aim was to wound and she didn't care what she said as long as she could hurt me. And she did.

I was the one who should have brought matters to an end, but I was too enamoured, or weak, or maybe just inexperienced in such matters. I swallowed her insults and kept visiting her, and occasionally a good time was had by all, as in the past, though it was usually followed by yet another row.

One night, when I went to see her, I was surprised to find a strange car parked outside the bungalow. My first reaction was to turn around and leave, but as I would have had to turn my car (I, of course, dismissed Kassim on these evenings) I reckoned my immediate departure would look even odder than my arrival, so I decided to brazen it out.

As I mounted the verandah steps someone came out of the front door. He wore a RAF uniform, cap at a jaunty angle, moustache. You know the sort, prototype of the pilot-hero made famous by a thousand gallant deeds in the coming war. We gazed at each other, then he grinned, gave me a mock salute and a huge wink and was gone. Not a word spoken.

What the fuck was I going on about, she asked me. Had she ever lied to me? Did I think I owned her? Hadn't she told me plainly just what I was getting into? What kind of stupid bugger was I? It was just one of those things. She never wanted to see me again. Bloody Irish fool. She was sick of me and my crybaby whining. It wouldn't be so bad if I wasn't such a wet rag in bed. Limp prick. What a bloody bore. Oh, fuck off, she was sick to death of me.

Next week I was summoned to KL. Another move,

this time to Singapore. A significant promotion. I was to move into the Education Department. Had word of my indiscretion reached my superiors? Probably not, or my promotion might never have come through. But then again, perhaps it did. Despite a tendency to stuffiness these were good men, kindly men, with whom I had always worked happily and whom I regarded as friends. Their inclination, if they thought I was getting into what they would have regarded as trouble, would be to extricate me.

So, I packed my bags and Kassim and I headed south for the big city. Primrose? Before I left a Chinese servant came to my house with a note: 'Heard the news. Good luck and thank you for everything. God bless. P.' That's all.

Thank you? At any rate, it was goodbye Primrose. George, her husband, stayed behind after the Japs occupied Malaya during the war. He was one of that small band of Europeans who went into the jungle with the Communist guerrillas, who fought the invader with tremendous courage, and then when the war ended switched from trying to kill the Nips to trying to kill us, their erstwhile allies.

There's something about the jungle, I don't know what, that makes those who enter it journey constantly and aimlessly through it. George, starving and racked with disease, moved endlessly from jungle camp to jungle camp, never so much as firing a shot in anger, and then vanished. Ten years later there are still stories going around that he was alive and living with the *sakai*. He was an only child and there were elderly parents, who pathetically continued to believe that he was still out there somewhere. They even visited Malaya in an effort to discover some word of him, but

146

at that time the jungles were no-go areas, where only soldiers and trackers could move, so they found out nothing.

Eventually it was discovered what had happened to him, from a guerrilla who had turned himself in. George had stumbled into a camp, hidden deep in the jungle, starving and suffering from God-knows-what-combination of tropical diseases. At first he was received well, but as time went on his Communist hosts became increasingly impatient with him. He lay around day after day, unable to contribute in any way either as a fighter or food gatherer. Maybe, too, they suspected him of being some sort of spy.

Night after night they hectored him about the evils of capitalism, the glorious future of a Marxist Malaya. Who knows how long it might have gone on for, if it were not for the fact that he had a revolver? One night they came to him in his hut and tried to take it off him. There was a scuffle. He was shot in the knee. It was as certain a death sentence as if it had been in the head. They simply let him lie there and, weakened already in that breeding ground for infection, with no medicines available, he was a corpse within a few days.

Poor sod, I think of him emaciated and dying on the floor of some smoky *attap* hut. What were his final thoughts? Home, his mother, his faithless wife? He is buried somewhere amid that vast greenery, where his grave can never be found.

Prim, I never saw again. I later heard that she got away to Australia in the débâcle of the fall of Singapore, and there she settled. I wonder, did she find much consolation there? At least it would have been warmer than Bournemouth. I wonder if she's still alive. If she is, her age would now be about . . . good God, she can't be!

Chapter Ten

SINGAPORE, THE Lion Gate, crossroads to the world, hub of the Empire. I found myself a beautiful house, high on a hill overlooking the city. Below me was the sea, dotted with tropical islands, and through the channels between them and the mainland passed the shipping of the world. Sampans and tankers, junks and liners, fishing boats and warships, every conceivable type and size of floating craft that man has devised, going or coming through the sea lines that joined the Pacific with the Indian Ocean, and which converged at this point.

After my day's work Kassim would pick me up and drive me home, where I would shower and sit in the huge bow window of my upstairs sitting room, looking down at my well-tended always flowering gardens and their green lawns, and further below at the unending stream of ships that passed towards the great harbour. I got to recognize the various lines from their livery. Blue Funnel, P&O, the Glen Line, the Bibby Line, the Dutch, the Japanese, the Americans.

I did not attempt to repeat my adventure with Primrose, which had left me somewhat ashamed of myself. More than that, the old Irish Catholic guilt feelings left me little peace. I had confessed my adulteries to a priest, with some trepidation, but he hardly seemed to have heard me, handing out a penance of three Hail Marys that left me, the great sinner, feeling rather resentful and short changed. I suppose he had to listen to worse every day of the week, or maybe he really didn't hear me, like the spectacularly deaf and bad-tempered curate who would sit in his confession box in our parish church when I was young, shouting, with mounting irritation: 'What? *What?* Speak up, will you?' until you were shouting your sins for the delectation of all those waiting outside to follow you.

Oh, those Arcadian days! But the world was changing beneath our feet, the volcano was giving off too much smoke. The great seventeen-inch guns of Singapore pointed out to sea from their emplacements, there were many more troops to be seen, searchlights stabbed the air and planes buzzed around the sky. All paper-thin defences, as it transpired, but to us they seemed consoling . . . no, not consoling for we needed no such consolation. They were, if anything, excessive, for who in the East could touch the Almighty, the eternal British Empire?

Not the Japanese, certainly, the epitome of a lesser breed, small, short-sighted and, we were told, afraid of the dark. How could they, the makers of cheap tin toys that fell apart in your hands, cope with the guns and planes of modern warfare? Their aircraft, it was said, were barely airworthy, manufactured from paper and old scrap, discarded kettles and used cars, the sort of things tinkers collected in Ireland. And, even if they got them off the ground, their notorious myopia would make it impossible for them to drop bombs with any accuracy, assuming, that is, that the bombs didn't first explode and kill their carriers. The reality, of course, was very different, but this nonsense was believed, not just by racist drunken planters in remote up-country clubs but by high-ranking military and civilian leaders.

Meanwhile this disciplined race cut our hair, picking up what gossip they could in their barber shops, fished (and mapped) the coasts, ran businesses that involved the repair of bicycles, one of their invading army's most useful weapons in the coming war, and went on picnics into the jungle, where they assiduously noted the where-abouts of tracks through the seemingly impenetrable foliage.

Once more I was due for leave and once more the problem of Eileen loomed. This time, I was determined that I would not be put off by her desire to avoid seeing me. You may have wondered why I have not mentioned her and Maurice for some time. The reason is that there was nothing to report. Then, one day, letters came from them both. Again, briefly, my heart gave a jump. Absurd, the letter was as cold as the last one, a financial report, business matters in which she seemed to be increasingly involved.

Oh, and Maurice. A request for increased fees now that he was going to boarding school. Yes, despite all her protestations about not being able to live without him she had sent him away. The justification, it seemed, was the low standard of the local Christian Brothers school, socially more than academically, I suspect, and (though she didn't say it in as many words) the fact that the child had no father. The boy himself wrote me occasional dutiful letters thereafter: 'Dear Daddy, I am enjoying school. We played Blackrock in the Schools Cup and lost ...'

Once I had got over my anger with her, I myself had written to her on several occasions and always made sure her allowance was paid on time, though being late with it was probably the surest way of hearing from her. I had mentioned the possibility of her joining me again, had once in a moment of more than ordinary loneliness pleaded with her. I had mentioned my various promotions, sent photographs of my splendid new home and told her of the urban attractions of Singapore. Nothing. No reply. I had gone through agonies of totally unfounded jealousy, imagining her with other men. But, inevitably, the wounds had healed. As the song says: What cannot be cured must be endured.

Then came the war in Europe and the deteriorating situation in the East. I was asked in by my immediate superior and requested to defer my leave, a request which I knew well I couldn't refuse. I wrote home to Eileen, to Maurice, to my brothers and sisters – only the last-named replied.

Shangri La! Singapore seems now like a dream. How could we have been so blind? While the bombs rained down on London we went to the Swimming Club, which boasted one of the biggest pools in the world, swam lazily in the warm water or in the oily sea in areas fenced off by stakes driven into the sand close together so that the sharks couldn't get in. Dressed to the nines, we attended charity balls in aid of the 'war effort' back home. Bombs. Thousands died. We played golf, tennis and cricket, or went to the films, Edward G. Robinson in *The Sea Wolf*, Bette Davis in *The Great Lie*. Noël Coward was probably right when he described Singapore as a first-rate place for second-rate people. I know he meant it in a different way, snobbishly, but I can't help including myself in it all the same.

Occasionally the boom of the big guns, firing at practice targets in the sea, reminded us of sterner things. But it was as if a collective blindness had taken hold. The Japs would never attack when it came to the crunch. As the tragedy moved inexorably forward I left Singapore and headed north on a tour. Part of my job was to visit schools and colleges, check on how they were doing, and confer with their principals about their problems.

It was a leisurely progress and, on the whole, a pleasant one. Many of these headmasters and mistresses were good people, but there was a disproportionate number of them whom the job had turned into petty tyrants with an inflated idea of their own importance and an attitude of disdain to their Asiatic teachers and pupils.

Most of all I was looking forward to seeing Tommy and Deirdre again. He was now in the state of Kedah in the north of the country. It was now three years since we had met, except for a Christmas spent in one of those hill stations where one went to get away from the heat. Their children had by now gone home to Ireland and boarding school, with an aunt caring for them during holidays. They were up near the border, where rubber from Malaya and buffalo from Thailand were smuggled, where both races carried long memories of disputed provinces, battles and real or imagined wrongs to Islam and Buddha.

It was splendid to see Tommy again, looking fit and well, but Deirdre had gone, sent south to Singapore with the other women and children 'just in case of trouble'. Just in case! On my first night, as I sat having dinner with Tommy in his bungalow, word came through on the radio that the Japs had landed at Singora in Thailand, not far away and at Kota Bahru on the east coast.

What happened next has been chronicled many times. The speed, the intelligence, the good training of the Japanese. The stupidity, over-confidence, bad equipment and lack of training of our side. The chaos, the lack of understanding of jungle warfare, the sheer bloody cock-up.

But back to my own experience. Next day we could hear firing in the distance, as the two armies engaged. We discussed whether we should move out, but the action seemed miles away and, in our innocence, we felt there was no rush. Tommy, too, was a member of a local unit of the army reserves, as were most of the Europeans by then, and was trying to find out where and when he should report for duty. But this meant a twenty-mile drive to the nearest town, as the telephone lines were down. We loaded up a truck and decided to move out the following day.

I was awakened before dawn by Kassim.

'*Tuan, tuan*, the Japanese are coming.'

I tumbled out of bed and pulled on my clothes. Tommy was in the living room, gulping down a cup of tea. 'Let's get the hell out of here,' he said.

I decided to abandon my car and, with Kassim and one of Tommy's boys driving, we headed south in the truck, away from the fighting. Not for long. After about a mile we rounded a corner to see ahead of us the shattered remains of a barricade and an armoured car which was still on fire. The bodies of six or seven men lay around in the grotesque poses of death – Punjabis, those that you could identify, except for a British officer who looked about nineteen.

How the blazes did the Japs get here, we wondered.

There was nothing we could do, so we determined to continue on our journey, when we heard a cry from the jungle fringes along the road. It was a European, a soldier from one of the Scottish regiments. His clothes were torn, he had a wounded arm, he was covered in sweat and mud, he looked feverish.

'Thank God,' he said. 'Here, sir, here.'

We went over to the edge of the road and saw he was not alone. Another young soldier lay there, semiconscious. He had a hole in his side that you could fit a cricket ball into and it was plain that he was dying. As we knelt beside him he gave a thin croak.

'Water,' he said, 'water.'

We gave him some from bottles we had brought with us, and tried to dress his wound with the few medical supplies we had – a futile gesture.

'Where's the front?' we asked.

There was no bloody front. The Japs had made their way through the jungle round the barricade and come up from the rear. The fight had been fierce but short. One armoured car had got away, or at least back down the road, everyone else had been killed or wounded. The Japs had finished off the wounded with their bayonets, except for the two now in front of us. The dying man had been either overlooked or it was decided he was dead already. The other had lain under a bush, face down, for two hours.

'No point going on by road,' said Tommy. 'The Japs are up ahead of us already. We'll have to cut across country.'

'Through the jungle?' asked the unwounded soldier in some alarm.

The average life-span of a British soldier in the jungle was said to be less than a week and though, mercifully, he didn't know that, he shared the general distrust felt by his comrades-in-arms of the country, its people and its food.

'There's no other way to go.'

'But what about Jack?' Jack croaked something inaudible. The flies were buzzing around his awful wound. We looked at each other.

'Well send help for him,' I said. Yes, yes. The others agreed to the lie. Impossible to move him through the jungle. Needed a doctor. We'd send help.

'*Tuan*!'

Kassim had heard something. We dived into the undergrowth fringing the road. We heard and then saw two Japanese motorcycles. They shot past without pause and the silence of a Malayan jungle day descended again.

'Come on, let's load up what we can and get out of here,' said Tommy.

We took little enough. A gun, some food, what was left of our medical supplies. Tommy's Chinese boy had vanished. Gone back to his people, wise man.

I put a bottle of water beside Jack, though he had hardly the strength to lift it to his mouth. As I turned to go he found his voice. Clearly.

'Please don't leave me,' he said.

We're going for help. You need a doctor. Not fit to travel through the jungle. Don't worry.

'Please don't leave me.' We turned to go. 'Please, please.'

We entered the jungle.

The fruit of the durian has the sweet, sour smell of decay. It pervades the flesh. It throws itself up like vomit from the stomach through the oesophagus, into the throat and the mouth.

There were four of us. Myself, Kassim, Tommy and the Scottish soldier, whose name I never knew.

Where were we heading, I asked Tommy.

'Campbell's place, almost due east of where we are now.'

'Campbell? Good God, he must be about a hundred years old by now.'

'Nearly eighty, anyway. He decided to stay on after retirement.'

'Good God.' Europeans weren't meant to live that long.

'We may be able to get some kind of transport there and link up with the army. His plantation is about twenty miles from here.'

Twenty miles, it doesn't seem far. A day, two if you take your time. But this was dense, primary jungle, without tracks. Five miles in a day would be good going. Three would be more like it. Tommy got out a compass. We pushed our way in. Thorns clawed at us. Branches struck us on the face and legs. Bushes surrounded us. The heat was like a stifling wet blanket. At first the Scottish soldier cursed and swore with a fluency that was almost poetic, but after a while even this became too much of an effort. His wound was superficial but was already turning septic. We dressed it. The rain came down like an avalanche, soaking us through to the very marrow. Under our feet mud churned up. We slid, we tripped over roots. A thorn like a hook tore my arm. Hour after hour passed, and we seemed to be getting nowhere.

We came to a river, it was small, but a torrent that crashed through some rocks at speed. We looked for a tree trunk, for some way to cross, but none could be found. We were so wet anyway that it hardly mattered.

I led the way in. In a few paces the water was up to my armpits, its force so strong that it threatened to take the legs from under me. There was a cry from the Scot as he was swept away.

'I can't swim,' he yelled, then he was off downstream.

Tommy dived after him. Two heads bobbing in the wild brown water. Kassim and I scrambled ashore and ran along the bank downstream. Another cry. The two of them were clinging to a rock. We got into the water again and managed to pull them to safety.

The four of us lay exhausted and drenched beside the river. We had lost most of our equipment, including our medical kit, our food and the soldier's rifle. The sun came out, burning, burning and dried us out. The leeches, attracted by the smell of blood, massed in bunches around the places where we had been scratched and cut and bitten.

We had nothing to get them off with. 'Don't break them off,' we told the soldier, but they filled him with such disgust that he did so, or as much as he could, leaving their hook-like heads to suppurate his flesh. Too tired to look for food or even erect shelters, we lay down for the night beside the river.

The darkness descended and the jungle chorus began with its whoops, whirrs, screeches, chatterings, howls. To these were added the ravings of the Scottish soldier, who, it was clear, had malaria or worse. He called on someone called Jessie. There was fluent cursing, violence, tears. A mother? A lover? What Glaswegian slum nightmare was running through his fevered brain?

We had all been through malaria in our time in the East. Indeed, in my early days there, it caused many deaths – there were so many things you could catch then that by the time it was diagnosed it was often too late. To this day I get occasional bouts of it, which leave me feverishly sweating until it breaks. Still, those of us who had been years in the East had probably built up some resistance to it, unlike the soldier who was undoubtedly new out from Europe. The only treatment for it, at that time, was quinine, and we had none.

Next morning he could barely walk. We took it in turns to support him and plunged into hell again. The jungle is not flat, at least not in Malaya. We climbed hills, we climbed what seemed like mountains. We slithered in red mud and fell on our faces. We grazed our knees and elbows, providing new feeding places for the leeches, which can creep up your body without you noticing and sink their fangs into your flesh without you feeling it, thanks to an anaesthetic they inject into your blood.

The soldier descended into insanity again. He collapsed, we lifted him up. Kassim, a lithe slender man like so many Malays, proved to be the strongest of us, virtually carrying the sick man for mile after mile. There was no food. We ate some berries which Tommy, with his jungle knowledge, claimed were all right. I got them down but the Scotsman, though he was in one of his more clear states, could only stomach a mouthful and then threw it up.

Finally after – how long? Days? Weeks? Time had no meaning any more – the jungle thinned and gave way to rubber trees. Campbell's bungalow, we reckoned, was on the other side of the hill, so we sent Kassim ahead to reconnoitre. While we waited for his return we slumped among the carefully spaced trees.

Our feet were blistered and swollen from the leech bites. My boots had split, our clothes were torn, jungle sores were breaking out on our bodies. The soldier lay there half-conscious, eyes half-open, hardly breathing.

'Hang on, old man,' said Tommy. 'Not far to go now.'

'Fuck it,' said the soldier.

Kassim returned. 'Nobody is there, *tuan*. Even the dogs have gone.'

We decided we'd take the chance of going in. There might be food. There might be quinine. There might be Japanese.

We struggled up the slope but had hardly gone twenty yards when the soldier fell again. He lay face down, and when we turned him over he was dead. We went on.

Kassim was quite right. Silence surrounded Campbell's bungalow. Gingerly we entered. It was the buzzing of the flies that told us where he was.

Campbell was still seated at the kitchen table, a service revolver in his hand. He had blown out his brains and had obviously been dead some time. An old man, the hair grey, plastered with blood and brains. Beside him, alive, sat a middle-aged Chinese woman, her face red and bloated with tears. The last of the sleeping dictionaries? She said nothing.

Death, death, death. It was everywhere in those days. We debated whether we should bury him, as the body was beginning to stink in the tropical heat, but had neither the strength nor the time to do so. Instead we carried him out, covered him with a tarpaulin we found and left him among the rubber trees which had been his life's work. When we went back into the bungalow the woman was gone. We searched the kitchen and found tins of pilchards and of prunes, which we wolfed down.

All I wanted to do was lie down on a bed and sleep, but Tommy said we must be off again. We packed what we could find in the line of supplies and, once more, were about to head for the jungle when we heard a motor. There was no time to take cover. I dived under a bed. Tommy and Kassim took to a large wardrobe.

Footsteps. Then an English voice said: 'Seems to be deserted.' I never heard a more welcome sound.

We emerged from our hiding places, like errant husbands discovered in a French farce. Two young officers confronted us. We must have made a sorry picture, even in better times a comical one.

'Good Christ,' one said, 'what have we here?'

We told our story and they theirs. They had been heading south in a staff car when a group of Chinese coolies signalled them to stop. They did so, but the coolies turned out to be disguised Japanese troops who opened fire. Their driver and another officer had been killed but the other pair had managed to shoot back and get away. They'd stopped at the bungalow for the same purpose as ourselves, to get food and water. Could they offer us a lift, they asked, as if we were going home from the Club.

I made a decision. 'Kassim,' I said, 'you must return to your *kampong*, it's not too far from here. If the Japanese catch you with us they will undoubtedly shoot you.'

'*Tuan*,' he said. 'You have treated me like a son. It is my duty to stay and serve you.'

'No, you have done your duty. Get back, find your wife and children, they'll need you. Go, and Allah be with you.'

I embraced him, he wept. I could see the army officers looking at me with raised eyebrows. He left and I was not to see him again until after the war. Tommy and I climbed into the back of the car and we drove off down the road towards Singapore.

Chapter Eleven

OWN THROUGH the war-torn peninsula we drove, against the flow of traffic that was heading towards the fighting. The British troops were dressed in smart uniforms, many of them carrying 40-pound packs on their backs in the tropical heat. They had heavy boots, water bottles, web equipment, tin hats, ground sheets – some of them even wore greatcoats. Their Japanese enemies wore a minimum of clothing, often no more than a singlet, shorts and tennis shoes. On their heads they wore handkerchiefs, knotted at their four corners, like you used to see people doing on a hot day at the seaside in Ireland. They rode bicycles, they carried a bag of rice, an ammunition belt, often a tommy-gun or a small mortar that did terrible damage. They were indifferent to death, quicker, smarter, deadlier in every way than we were.

Our chauffeur, Kendall, was a young subaltern who, with his companion, was headed for Singapore. I didn't think it proper to ask him on what important military mission he was bent, but he confided to us anyway during one of our many interminable stops to let convoys of military vehicles pass us.

'My CO,' he said, 'is the meanest man in the army. Rented a house in Singapore. We were sent up to the front in a hurry and when we got there he got worried

162

about the native servants. I'm being sent back to read his gas and electricity meters, in case they've been leaving the lights on all night and cooking meals for their pals. Can you credit it?'

His companion, Shortt, had, he told us, 'wangled himself a spot of leave' to visit his financée, the daughter of one of Singapore's wealthy merchant families. I never discovered what influence he had, to get away from the fighting in the first days of a war.

Though the signs of disintegration were already all around us, both viewed the conflict with unabashed optimism. Their only regret, they told us, was that they were not fighting a 'real enemy', particularly the Germans. The Nips, said Kendall, were basically an uninteresting race, it was difficult to work up any real heat about them. Soon the British forces would steady themselves, hold the line and then thrust the blighters back into the sea. Is it any wonder that the Japanese showed such contempt for the white man?

We slept overnight in the car, our exhaustion overcoming the discomfort, and next day, after another long drive, we crossed the causeway which linked the Malay state of Johore with Singapore island. Our drivers were to leave us off at (where else?) Raffles Hotel, and I remember us passing some tennis courts where a mixed doubles, clad in immaculately laundered whites, was at play. Singapore was still like a sleep-walker, half aware of approaching danger but unable to do anything about it.

While the young soldiers and I had the inevitable *stengahs*, Tommy got on the phone and soon Deirdre was with us, as welcome, as pretty and as reassuring as always. She had had the chance, she told us, to take passage on a ship bound for Australia, but had refused this escape, preferring to wait for her husband and myself. She was amazingly cheerful and optimistic about the outcome of the war in Malaya, as indeed we all were.

Looking back, it all seems so unreal. The idiotic presumption of eventual victory, the determination to go on with life as if nothing had happened, the stifling red tape that, time and again, prevented any decisive action. Things changed, of course – bit by bit, disaster by disaster, our smugness was eroded. The three of us headed back to my house and waited to see what the future would bring.

The island city of Penang fell, disgracefully. The once all-powerful *tuans* pulled out without a fight after only a week of war. British residents were told to get ready for evacuation. The last couple of ferry boats were put at their disposal and they sailed off in ignominy, taking with them six (six!) of the five hundred Asiatic volunteers, who had been preparing to fight for King and Empire.

To the native population, who saw their brothers and sisters left helpless to cope with the advancing Japanese army, it was an act of gross betrayal. Was this the invincible, the all-wise white man, the strong but just father, stern in battle, honourable, brave? To them we had ratted on our promises, turned tail like cowards the moment things started to get hard, and left the lesser breeds to suffer and die. Things could never be quite the same between us thereafter.

Back and back went the British army. In Singapore morale fell slowly. Every day the bombers came over in seemingly increasing numbers. There were no air-raid shelters, the authorities having decided that the ground was too swampy for underground constructions.

The safest, indeed the only places to take cover from the bombs if you were caught in the open, were the open concrete sewers which lined every street. About a foot wide and three feet deep, they were not the most inviting hideaways, but at least they gave you some chance of surviving as you crouched amongst the rats and the excrement, a handkerchief over your mouth to ward off the foul smell. I remember during one raid seeing an Indian slip and fall in, breaking his leg in the process, an accident which caused the onlookers to roar with laughter.

Rumour ran rife. Everybody seemed to know a man who'd talked to a man who'd seen German Luftwaffe pilots, captured after being shot down over Malaya. Fifth-columnists were behind every tree, it was believed, guiding in the enemy bombers with flashlights or blowing up buildings. Huge forces of reinforcements were on their way and squadron upon squadron of the latest planes.

For Tommy and me there was a curious lull. Because education had virtually ceased to exist I had little work to do. We volunteered for various tasks, such as helping to clear up after the bombings, but even here we were hindered as the Chinese coolies who were meant to do the actual donkey work tended to go absent more and more. Deirdre was busier, working in one of the hospitals coping with the aftermath of the raids, in which hundreds were dying.

I remember once being caught in an open area when the sirens went off. I lay down in a shallow ditch, the only available cover, ruining my white suit. Lying on my back, I could see the approaching planes and realized that the bomb run would be right over me. A couple flopped down beside me, a young naval officer and his very pretty girl.

The planes were almost overhead and suddenly I could see them shedding a succession of black dots – the bombs! As they fell I could see them getting bigger. I felt hypnotized. Was this the end of it all? The bombs fell in a line. There was a thudding in the earth as the first struck, some distance away, the second was nearer, another nearer still. The thudding in the earth got louder each time. Nearer, nearer, my God, to thee.

The ground rocked, heaved, the noise deafened me. I knew this was the end. I tried to tunnel into the ground. There was the roar of anti-aircraft fire, the crash of houses collapsing, windows shattering. I was terrified, I was numbed. Then it stopped and there were no more bombs. I peeped up, the planes were flying away, the firing stopped, the raid was over.

Myself, the officer and the girl stood up. We were covered in dust, she was shaking uncontrollably.

'That was a close one,' I said.

He nodded curtly, but made no reply. Dammit, we'd never been introduced.

Closer and closer came the Japs, more and more bizarre became the situation. Christmas Day came and Tommy, Deirdre and I played host to a motley collection of fellow civil servants and some military personnel, including a young Irish RAF pilot. He flew a Brewster Buffalo, one of the few fighters available to defend us from the enemy air attacks – even the name seems faintly comical. The ungainly and outmoded flying Buffalo could not even get high enough to attack the Jap bombers, and even if it could have it took so long to get off the ground that they had usually done their business and departed by the time it had arrived at the scene of action.

Riordan, our guest that day, was eventually shot

down and killed, like virtually all his fellow pilots, probably the victim of a Japanese Zero, a flying machine we had scorned as made of paper and gum, but which was actually as good and better than most of the planes of the Second World War.

Kuala Lumpur, the federal capital, fell. There was a major pull-back of the British forces. And then the enemy was at the gates. The last remaining troops straggled back across the Causeway which links Singapore island with the mainland of Malaya and on 31 January, a fine sunny day, we heard the explosion as it was blown up.

And so one million people, crowded together, faced the approaching conquerors. There was a brief lull while the army tried to patch together, in a few days, defences that had been neglected for years, and looked uneasily across to the mainland where the Japanese were now plainly visible. Meanwhile, life went on. Women had their hair done, long queues formed outside the cinemas, the shops were open and doing well as people stocked up with food and drink, clothes and books. People went out to dinner, swam at the swimming club, played bridge and went dancing.

A week later the Japanese landed on the island in the darkness. The strait, according to the British plan, was to be brilliantly lit up by searchlights as soon as the enemy was sighted, but they were never switched on, as every line of communication to headquarters had been cut by bombing and no one could or would act without orders from the top. More bungling. We could hear the fighting, intense, savage and getting nearer.

Next day we awoke to find that the servants had all gone. We had no transport as I had lost my car fleeing from the Japs in the north, and anyway it was becoming almost impossible to get hold of petrol. We were stuck some miles out of town and didn't know what to do. It was clear that total surrender was only a question of time. A horn sounded outside the house. It was Morgan, a colleague from the MCS, and by some miracle he had a car that was still going.

'I hear the navy is still taking off women and children down at the docks,' he said. 'Care to give it a try?'

Tommy and I looked at each other. Why not?

'No,' said Deirdre. 'I want to stay with you.'

'Darling,' said Tommy. 'I think you should go. God knows what will happen if the Japs take the city.'

'I'll take that chance,' she said.

'Look,' I said, 'even if we come through all this and end up prisoners, you won't be together. They'll put the women in separate camps.'

'I don't want to go,' she said.

Tommy put his arms around her. 'Think of the boys,' he said.

'Look,' said Morgan. 'We've got to get cracking if you want to do this. There's no time to be lost.'

We drove through the wrecked city, through the slaughtered streets. Dead bodies, the victims of air raids, were lying everywhere. Smoke hung in the air. At one point the gutters were running in whiskey where the authorities had ordered the contents of a warehouse to be destroyed. Looters staggered out of shops carrying impossible loads of everything under the sun. Splintered telegraph poles stood at drunken angles, their wires trailing on the ground. Bomb craters blocked the way. People were everywhere, fleeing from the wrath to come, their belongings on their backs, in rickshaws, handcarts, or, in one case, carried in an empty coffin by two men.

At the docks crowds of Europeans hung around the waterfront. There were still a few destroyers coming and going, bringing cargoes of refugees out of the doomed city. They sent launches ashore to pick up people and every time one of these was signalled there was a desperate, panicky rush to get aboard. Men as well as women were trying to get away. When the chips were down the sons and daughters of the Empire were behaving badly.

Deirdre clung to Tommy's arm as we waited, clutching the small bag that she had hurriedly packed in her other hand. A pinnace had put out from one of the destroyers moored about a hundred yards offshore. The waiting group pushed forward towards the steps that led down from the quay to a slippery landing place. Oily waters lapped the steps, unspeakable detritus floated in the slapping waves. We joined the throng thrusting forward, holding Deirdre between us to keep her steady.

'Excuse me,' said a heavy middle-aged woman. 'Excuse *me*! I was here first, I should have been on the boat last time. Stand aside!'

'Oh, shut up, Mildred,' said the man beside her.

The launch drew nearer. The crowd started to shout, meaninglessly, needlessly.

'Steady on, now. Steady!' shouted an officer in white ducks on board. 'One at a time, please!'

We were jostling, heaving, trying to keep our footing on the slippery steps. A man came charging down on the outside. An elbow caught him and he fell into the filthy waters. No one paid any attention. We got to the bottom of the steps with Deirdre. The boat was almost full and the crowd was pressing behind us. I put my hand on the shoulder of a woman behind me and held her off, while Tommy handed his wife aboard.

'Bastard,' said the woman. 'You absolute bastard!'

We stood back and let the last few aboard. The boat pulled away, Deirdre lifted a hand in mute farewell. On the quay the woman who said she'd been there first was weeping.

Tommy, Morgan and I stood silently as the destroyer got under way and watched till it passed out of sight. Then we heard the drone of approaching aircraft. The crowd on the quay scattered, making for the big warehouses there, which offered the only possible shelter. We jumped out of our car and ran after them. A bomb burst a hundred yards or so away and a group of trucks and lorries went up in flames.

We looked back and saw Morgan. He had stopped and was heading back towards his car, for the flames from the other vehicles were approaching it.

'Come back!' shouted Tommy. But Morgan was already behind the wheel and driving the car to safety. As he did the bombers, which had passed overhead, wheeled and came back for a second run. He drove towards the shelter of a warehouse and pulled up, but as he did so a bomb exploded across the street. I saw him slump over the wheel, and ran towards him. Blood poured from his chest where he had been hit by a shower of shrapnel. He was dead.

The bombers left. It was a beautiful day. The smoke kept off the sun and made the air cool, so that it was like a Mediterranean spring. We loaded Morgan's body into the back of the car, I got into the blood-stained driver's seat and we headed back the way we had come.

We buried him on the lawn of my beautiful garden, marking his grave with a wooden cross. We decided to stay where we were thereafter, for at least we were away from the city centre. The bombings were now constant and, though they seemed indiscriminate, at least we'd be away from the areas where they were heaviest.

Tommy said some prayers, as many as he could remember from the funeral service, and as we turned away from the grave we heard a car pull up. It was an officer I had never seen before. Tears of grief and indignation were in his eyes.

'Did you hear?' he asked. 'We've surrendered! Bloody surrendered! We hadn't even begun to fight!'

That evening we dined on tins of sardines and asparagus, washed down with whiskey, and talked late into the night about Ireland, our lives, our wives, our children, our childhoods, about all the things close friends talk about, and all the things they don't need to talk about. We talked, in short, about everything but the immediate future.

Chapter Twelve

S O SINGAPORE fell and with it the British Empire. Yes, the war would be won, the *tuans* would return, and the Japs would make themselves so hated during their occupation that we would be warmly welcomed back. But it could never be the same again. The long decline was coming to an end. That infuriating assumption of superiority which is Britain's trademark would live on, but with less and less grounds for it, and, underneath, there would be a loss of confidence dating back to that stunning defeat in 1942 to which I was a witness.

Meanwhile, there was dismay and horrified incredulity. To those who supported the Allied cause it was a calamity, a catastrophe. Back home in Ireland, I am told, it was greeted with jubilation by a sizeable section of the population. Any defeat of the old enemy was to be welcomed, and this one was made doubly sweet by the fact that the inept British commander, Percival, had served with the hated Auxiliaries in Ireland during the Black and Tan war of the twenties.

We saw our first Nips up close next morning. Clad in their jungle-green uniforms and peaked caps, they looked a mild enough bunch. Then we heard that the defeated soldiers had orders to march to Changi Gaol, a vast grim complex of buildings on the east of the island, though not vast enough for the eighty thousand or so men who would now be incarcerated there. The rest of the male civilians – some two and a half thousand of us – were assembled some days later, and followed the military to Changi.

What must the native population have thought as they saw us, their former masters, march past? An impossible question, though certainly they behaved better to us than we had to them. Few of them were on the street, and those that were turned their backs as we passed. But it was clear that this was not a gesture of rejection; rather one designed to show that they wanted nothing to do with the whole stinking mess. For all our faults few of the many peoples of this heterogenous land hated us, or wished us ill. But we needed no jeers, no one laughing at our plight to feel the humiliation of it all.

And so began our Agony in the Garden, our Way of the Cross, for some of us our Crucifixions. As far as the people at home in Britain and Ireland were concerned, it was as if we had vanished into the jaws of hell itself, in great clouds of smoke and flame like an army of Don Giovannis. From the chaos of Fallen Singapore little or no news came of who had lived, who had died, who was wounded, who intact. Wives and widows, no one knew which was which.

Deirdre Evans, who was to spend the rest of the war in Australia, told me later that it was two years before she had any word of Tommy. Then one day, through the post, came a small dirty, stained Red Cross postcard. On it was printed a single sentence, 'I am alive and a prisoner in . . .' Tommy had filled in 'Singapore' and signed his name. She wept tears of joy that day, but it might have been better if she had never got it.

173

As far as I was concerned I was in a bit of a spot as to whom I should send my postcard – we were only allowed one. Should it go to my son, whom I didn't know, or my wife, who didn't want to know me? I settled for my sister. It, too, got through and she told me she brought it to Eileen, who thanked God and dabbed her eyes briefly with her hankie.

I'm glad I only found that out years later. In the camp, where sentimentality and fantasy were part of every day, my imagination would have got to work on the scene and a full-blooded reconciliation would have formed itself in my head – some hope!

How to describe captivity? The boredom, interspersed with terror, the sense of hopelessness, of failure, the disease, dysentery, beri beri, yaws, fever of different kinds, the discomfort, the bed bugs, the stinging ants, the cockroaches, the heat, the back-breaking work.

All of these things, but first came hunger. It never left you: when you woke up, as you fell asleep. You dreamed of roast beef, potatoes and butter, cakes, soda bread, bacon and eggs, anything, everything. You got a few handfuls of low-grade rice, full of pieces of grit, occasionally a piece of fish, often rancid, or some vegetable matter – you could hardly call them vegetables.

This was no European prisoner-of-war camp, surrounded by guards and barbed wire and searchlights to prevent escape. Where could we escape to, anyway? In Singapore, hawkers called round to the camps, offering food for sale. To pay them you borrowed from money lenders. (Yes, we had them in the camp too, it was a regular little city. At the end of the war they sent in their bills, complete with monumental interest. The government declared that we needn't pay, but I did so all the same. Without them I would not have survived.)

Our empty stomachs made us selfish, cunning. We squabbled over pieces of garbage, we hoarded and bartered and cheated when we could. We tried to be disciplined, to behave in a civilized way, but hunger kept dragging us down.

Depression was a constant. We worried about families at home and about friends who were missing. We worried, too, about ourselves, what was our sentence – a few years, a lifetime, as our guards weren't slow to tell us?

We tried to organize our lives into some sort of routine. Church services, a library, concerts, classes and lectures – 'Birds of the Malay Peninsula', 'The Contemporary Theatre', 'The History of Ireland'. (Contentious that, as always, when I gave it. Two prisoners from Belfast walked out, protesting loudly at my nationalist views. How ridiculous to bring our local squabbles across the world to a Japanese POW camp, how incomprehensible and stupid it must have seemed to our fellow prisoners.)

It might all have been just bearable – tedious, dispiriting, but bearable – were it not for two things, the work and our captors. Tommy and I were put to digging trenches. In the merciless oriental sun it was backbreaking, exhausting labour for middle-aged Europeans. A moment's pause meant a blow from the guards, or sometimes a full beating, and we were never fast enough. 'Speedo, speedo!' they would shout, running towards us with bayonets fixed. Water was in short supply and there was hardly a respite from digging from start to finish of the day, when we would stagger back to our huts to eat our few mouthfuls, half falling with exhaustion. It was this, the doctors tell me, that gave me my dicky heart.

The Japanese who had taken Singapore were

fighting troops and though they despised our failure to give our lives in battle or, failing that, to kill ourselves, at least they had some fellow feeling with other soldiers. But they were soon moved on to other theatres of war. Those who replaced them were of a lower grade, stupid and brutal. Many of them were Koreans. Despised and ill-treated by the Japs, they took it out in turn on us, like the man who, having been shouted at by his superior, kicks his dog.

Not all of them were bad. Some were even kind, I suppose, turning a blind eye when we took rests, or agreeing to barter with us for goods or food, for they were nearly as poor and as badly fed as we were. Even the worst of them, as I was to find, could have their good moments. We gave them nicknames, Billy the Kid, Donald Duck, the Ice Cream Man, George Formby, based on how they looked and sounded, and made fun of them behind their backs, even while fearing them.

With them, too, came the Kempeitai, the Japanese secret police, who, according to camp gossip had taught their methods to the Gestapo. Certainly few could have surpassed them in sadism. Most of their efforts were directed against Asiatics suspected of being sympathetic to the old regime, and the torture chambers and graves of Singapore were full of their victims.

Their main concern with the prisoners was to find hidden radios, of which there were certainly quite a few – 'canaries' we called them. The parts were smuggled in in all sorts of ingenious ways, hidden in sacks of rice, under carts, even in water bottles. Once assembled they were constantly moved around so that they could not be discovered.

Donald Duck was a sergeant, so-called because of

his quacking way of talking and a set of buck teeth that reminded one of a beak. He was a mean one, too, quick to use the boot or the fist. Maybe these had been just as callously used on him by his own superiors... I am trying to be fair, God knows why. '*Kura*!' he would yell – a crude way of telling you to jump to it, and if you delayed an instant, or failed to bow to him you could be sure of at least a slap in the face.

I remember it so well, when I have forgotten so much. It comes to me in my dreams. Tommy saying to me, 'There's a canary in one of the huts.'

'Where?' I asked.

'You don't want to know, old boy.'

'Any news?'

'There's fighting in Burma. The Nip advance has been held. The Yanks have fought a big sea battle, a lot of Jap carriers have been sunk. Maybe things are beginning to turn round.'

I remember that.

We lived in a ramshackle hut, about fifteen of us, sleeping on makeshift beds of planks. The Nips must have picked up traces of the radio, but couldn't pin down its exact whereabouts.

They burst in early one morning while we were still asleep, shouting, kicking us awake. We stood, almost naked, each beside his bed. There were five of them, including Donald Duck and a Kempeitai officer with a samurai sword almost as long as himself.

'*Kirray*!' (Salute) roared Donald and we did so. The Kempetai officer barked something and the rest of them started to tear apart our beds, rip open our kit bags and scatter our meagre belongings all over the floor, kicking and cuffing anyone who got in the way.

The officer said something we did not understand,

except for the word 'radio', or, as he put it in the Japanese manner of adding a vowel to the end of words, 'Radioro'.

'Radioro, radioro,' shouted Donald Duck.

Nobody replied. He strode to the end of the hut, acting the part, as we thought, of the efficient underling for the benefit of the impassive secret service man.

'Engrishu no goodera,' he shouted. 'Damme, damme. Radioro finish, all men bang bang.'

Which meant, more or less, that the English were no good, and when they found the radio we would all be shot.

Going down the line, he stopped in front of each of us. As he did so we each bowed, knowing that not to do so would result in the inevitable blow in the face. I was third in the line, Tommy next after me. The first two got no more than a cursory look. He stopped in front of me for a long moment. I felt a knot of fear in my stomach. Then he bent down and picked something up from my odds and ends on the floor. It was a small black and white snapshot of Eileen and Maurice, aged about three, squinting into the sun, the little boy holding a ball, frozen in a long-forgotten moment.

'You chirren?' asked Donald Duck.

My mouth was dry. I nodded wordlessly. He reached into a back pocket and took out a wallet from which he extracted another photograph, which he showed me. It was himself, posing in uniform with a woman in Japanese dress. Beside them, shaven-headed, were two other small boys. They were also dressed in some sort of military uniform.

'Me ni chirren,' (I have two children) said Donald Duck, smiling. I did my best to smile back, my knees felt weak.

He handed back my photo and we bowed to each other like two courteous gentlemen.

I had hardly begun to feel relief when he turned to Tommy with a yell. Two soldiers ran forward and started to drag him from the hut. As he went he stumbled. They kicked him to his feet and dragged him out.

'No! No!' I said, but he was gone. The silent Kempeitai officer looked at us impassively and followed them out.

Why was he chosen – Tommy? Why not me, or one of the others? I have asked myself a thousand times. Why not me? Did they know something? Did someone inform? Or was it blind chance, ill luck? Was it destiny? Had his time run out? It should have been me. I had nothing to lose but my life, and that was mine alone. I should have offered myself in his place. But that photograph had saved me.

A car drove him away to some grim room with bloodstained walls in the city. Donald Duck, my saviour, went with him and the Kempeitai. He was, I was told after the war, a very artist of torture, imaginative, creative, obsessive in his devotion to the work in hand and to getting things perfectly right.

Shall I describe to you these desecrations, these horrors? The beatings with clubs and metal rods, the holding of heads under water until the prisoners were on the brink of drowning, the electric wires to the genitals, the sticking of hose pipes down a man's throat, filling him with water and then jumping on his stomach, the hanging upside-down over fires, the . . . no, what does it matter, what will it avail? They've all been described before, anyway. For a time I used to pore over them. Accounts of torture, trials of war criminals.

I found I was becoming obsessive, morbid about them. One day I put them all in the rubbish bin. Besides, the techniques were crude and have been far surpassed in these technologically wonderful times.

Suffice it to say that men were driven to death in that grim building. And for what? A few crackly wirelesses that occasionally spelt out a bulletin about the war which was probably half lies anyway, and that didn't make the slightest difference to either the prisoners or their guards, who wouldn't have believed it even if they could have understood what was being broadcast.

But, of course, that wasn't what it was about, was it? It was a question of face. Was the white enemy, who had been defeated and had further disgraced himself by choosing imprisonment rather than death, to be allowed to get one up on his captors, the new lords of the East? And, on our side, were these little monsters to be allowed their way yet again? Was that a cause worth dying for? Apparently, for not a few died for it eventually on both sides.

He was gone for three days, then they returned him. At first the Japs had been content to torture their chosen suspects to death and then send the bodies back to us for burial, but as time went on they would come back to us alive, just about. Why did they do this? Perhaps they felt that the war wasn't going as well as it had been, that a day of reckoning was coming and that somehow or other they'd be blamed less if they hadn't actually given the quietus.

As we sat around on the third day the door of the hut opened and he was thrown in on to the floor. His mouth was caked with blood, on which flies made a feast. An arm was broken and hung at a horrible angle.

His fingers had each been broken singly with a hammer, but not before bamboo shoots had been put under his nails and they had been levered off. His body had been kicked and beaten, he had internal injuries.

Almost worse, he had been left in the tropical sun for a whole day without water. Eventually he had dragged himself to a lavatory and drunk the water from the bowl. Even if the Japs had not killed him that water probably would have. He had then tried to throw himself out of an upstairs window, but was pulled back.

There were witnesses, survivors (there are always survivors) of the torture chamber, who later gave evidence at a war crimes trial. Some of the torturers were hanged.

He had told them nothing, given nothing away, said the survivors. Why? Because he knew nothing? Why not? He was a dead man once he was driven away in that car, food for worms as Shakespeare calls it. If he had confessed, others, too, might have died. But then, he might have been spared some of his agonies. Just a short, sharp chop. Morbid. I am morbid, dwelling on things best forgotten. But I cannot forget.

We rushed to pick him up. He didn't know where he was or who he was.

'*Air*,' he said, '*air*' (the Malay word for water).

We put the water to his lips. He coughed up blood and water. Get the doctor, send for the doctor.

'Coming out of the jungle,' said Tommy. 'Dark . . . night falling . . . dark . . . go on . . . what's there?' He shrieked in Malay, '*Ta'mahu, ta'mahu!*' (Don't want, don't want.)

'It's all right, old boy, it's all right,' I said. 'I'm here.'

'Damn mosquitoes.' He gave a cry of pain.

'Our Father, who art in heaven . . .'

181

'Where are they?'

'Hallowed be Thy . . . what?'

He knew me. 'Tim,' he asked, 'am I dying?'

'Hold my hand. Hold my hand, Tommy. The doctor's coming. Hold on, hold on.'

'Where are they now?' he asked. 'Where are they now, the boys of the old brigade? Under the spreading chestnut . . . remember? Remember, Tim?'

'Remember what? Deirdre?'

'Remember College? Football, football . . . Your brother Mick, some player!'

'Yes. I remember.' (Where's the bloody doctor?)

'Remember the year we won the cup? And the Sultan's wives were there with tigers. Tigers in the Istana, and we won.'

'Shh, easy.'

'Feet, College, feet!' He gave a cry: 'Garryowen! Garry—.' His mouth fell open, his head fell back. His eyes gazed into nothing.

The fruit of the durian is foul, strange. It has the foul stink of the charnel-house, the nauseating taste of the alien.

Garryowen, up and under! Tommy Evans and I first met when we were both twelve. He was the only Protestant in the school, Church of Ireland. His father had sent him to the Brothers, rather than have him travel across town to the only school in the place for his own kind. We could hardly have been more different. He was short, I was tall. He was fair, I was dark. He was steady, hard-working and hadn't a trace of imagination, I lazy, erratic and a dreamer. We were friends from the first day we met, and it was because of him that I first got the idea of going into the Colonial Service. We stayed friends for thirty-five years. He was an excellent scholar, a model pupil. The Brothers, I think, had the idea of converting him to Catholicism. What fools we are. A lifetime of observing most of the major religions has convinced me that there's precious little difference between any of them.

We buried him in the dusty prison graveyard, a place where as our years and months of captivity lengthened the wooden crosses sprouted and multiplied as if in a forest. A vicar prayed over him without warmth, even cursorily. I wept, but not much. I was numbed, but in the dead of night I felt a depth of desolation I had never known, not even when our baby died and Eileen left me. Again I felt utterly alone.

Months passed, years passed. Things slowly started to get better. In 1944, the civilians were moved from Changi to Sime Road, a camp where existence, though hard, was better than it had been. The canaries still sang their illicit songs in the camps and, though we could never be sure, the tide of war seemed definitely to be changing. Most encouraging was the appearance in the sky of American Flying Fortresses, huge (to our eyes) gleaming planes that bombed the Singapore docks and caused us to cheer wildly.

Better still, our captors started to treat us better. There were fewer blows, work became more and more cursory. But we were in a bad way. We had become sallow, hollow-eyed and gaunt, though we only noticed it after the war was over when our liberators all looked pink and plump.

Then, dramatically, it was all over. High in the sky a single American plane flew past and out of it came a lone parachute. As we watched, it drifted down, right into the middle of our parade ground. He was like a creature from another planet in his flying suit, boots and sun-glasses. An all-American tough guy straight out of the cinema – James Cagney or George Raft. A Japanese guard came running, bayonet at the ready. Stepping deftly out of the way, the Yank tripped him up, pulled him to his feet and barked something in fluent Japanese, sending him on his way with a kick in the arse. Then he lit himself a cigar. Five minutes later an officer turned out the guard. Salutes were exchanged as we stood watching with open mouths.

'What are you doing here?' somebody asked, stupidly.

'Jesus!' he said. 'Don't you guys know the war's over?'

You could hear the cheering spread from hut to hut. It's all a blur. Someone started singing, 'God Save the King', but no one could remember the words. The Japs vanished from view. I remember some of us going to the cold storage. It was still packed with food, including rations sent for us by the Red Cross and never given to us, though it was unpalatable to the Japs. I fried a pound of sausages in a pound of butter and was sick after I ate them. My stomach couldn't take it.

There were disgraceful episodes, of which little was said. Some of the most brutal guards were cornered and beaten to death. Among them was Donald Duck. I sometimes wonder about his wife and children in Japan. Were they as remote from him as were my family, whose photograph had saved me from poor Tommy's fate? Somehow I doubt it, but who's to know?

One thousand, two hundred and ninety-seven days had passed since Singapore fell and now we were going home. My feelings were overwhelming, yet mixed. First of all, they say, comes self-preservation and it was as if a colossal weight had been lifted off me, a weight of fear that had become so constant over the years of captivity that I was hardly aware of it. How long would the war last, would we ever be released, would one catch some disease, many of which were lethal with no proper medical treatment available, what fresh Japanese brutality might one encounter? (A well-founded fear, this last, for there were camps elsewhere in which machine-guns had been turned on the prisoners as defeat drew near for their captors.) Then there was the joy of freedom, of being able to go where you wanted, welcomed by the Chinese and Malay populations as we walked around the city, and were showered with gifts.

But with all this joy there came, too, moments of black despair, which would hit me in the middle of the night – they still do, indeed. Then my thoughts would turn to Tommy and his terrible end, and to the years that had passed so quickly, to Eileen, to Deirdre and to a lifetime spent in a country which would never again be the same. To anyone who experienced the war directly, I think it was as if they had three lives. Before the war, the war and after the war. Each a completely different world.

Small, everyday things, the sight of a child, a snatch of popular music, could reduce me to tears. I would giggle inanely at silly jokes, or get irritated with people for no good reason. I think most of us ex-prisoners of war were like this at first.

Then I was setting sail again for Ireland. Our packed troopship docked in Liverpool, and we found we were heroes. Bands played, flags flew as we drove in lorries along streets jammed with cheering people. I stood, I remember, beside another ex-prisoner wearing one of those wide-brimmed Australian hats with one side turned up. Suddenly there was a commotion. 'Johnny,' a woman's voice screamed. 'Johnny! It's my husband.' Our lorry stopped and she was pushed out of the watching crowd. Helping hands pulled her up into the lorry and she threw herself with a wild abandon into the arms of her companion. I wept as I had not wept in all my years of captivity. A sentimental moment.

A few days later I landed at Dun Laoghaire on a cold autumnal evening. My brother and sisters were waiting at the pier, and several of my nephews and nieces. How strange I must have looked to them in my coarse ill-fitting bits of various army uniforms, down to seven stone from my usual twelve or thirteen, yellow skin and ill-cut grey hair. Yet here, too, I was a hero. Ireland had suffered little in the war, but shared the general relief that it was over, and the feeling that new beginnings were possible. Old friends whom I had not seen for many years invited me to their homes, newspapers sent reporters to enquire about my experiences, complete strangers shook me by the hand and welcomed me home.

I luxuriated in things like sleeping in a real bed in a room by myself, eating real potatoes, sitting by a fire or walking in the cool green countryside. Yet, as time passed and the first joy of freedom faded, I felt a bitterness that I could hardly define. What had it been for? Why had I escaped? Who could know what had happened? Who would remember those who lay in the well-tended war graves? What did they die for? What did the Japanese die for? The world would take a few more turns and it would be as if we never were . . . But when was it or would it ever be any different?

I visited Maurice in his Jesuit boarding school. I drove along a long avenue off a country road and approached a castellated building with a chapel beside it, once the home of a Catholic family who had lost it in the aftermath of the Jacobite wars.

A butler showed me into a gleaming parlour, adorned with portraits of eminent past pupils, judges, leaders of the old Irish Party, archbishops and, yes, some colonial governors of the last century. It spoke of the old world of Irish nationalism which was swept aside in the 1916 Rising and its aftermath, when Sinn Fein cast the parliamentarians who had sat in Westminster out of office and won independence by violent means. Of the new men, the former IRA gunmen and politicians of 1916 and the twenties who were now government ministers, there was no sign. They had, in the main, come from slightly lower down the social ladder. But their sons were well represented among the present pupils of the school and, no doubt, their pictures too would adorn these walls in their own time.

He was a tall boy, his face well acned, his wrists protruding from the school blazer he had outgrown, gawky, coltish, shy, at that stage which can be both infuriating and oddly affecting. He came into the room and even then it was a shock to realize he was my son. We had then, as now, little to say to each other. We walked around the immaculately kept playing fields and through the ornamental wood, which stood beside the school. I prattled on, foolishly, in the way one does when one is with someone who makes no response to what one is saying. What had he been told about me? What did he himself think? I shall never know.

Our embarrassment was ended by the arrival of one of his teachers, a saturnine Jesuite priest. He greeted me civilly but with that edge of irony I have found so often among the members of his order. A cold fish. My son, he told me, was clever but could work harder, was average at games and fitted well into the life of the school. He spoke, with seeming approbation, of missionaries and of former pupils now working in Africa and Asia, yet managed somehow at the same time to convey an atmosphere of faint disapproval of the whole idea of Irishmen being involved in such matters. Someone told me later that he had been in Spain at the time of the civil war there, a devout admirer of Franco, and had been forced to leave because of some British government intervention – something for which he never forgave Winston Churchill. From him the wrong side had won the world war.

I took Maurice out to a nearby town, filled him with cakes and tea and sent him back with more money than I should have given him. He left me with no discernible sign of regret.

I met Deirdre, who had spent most of the war in Australia. She too, had had adventures after the destroyer had taken her away from Singapore. She had been transferred to a merchant ship, which was bombed and sunk while it was at anchor off one of the many little islands around the coast. Half of those on board were killed by the bombs or drowned trying to get ashore. Deirdre was luckier. A good swimmer, she made it to the island, an uninhabited piece of coral, jungle and sand with hardly any water. There, over six hundred people, many of them badly wounded, huddled together, thirsty, starving and in terror of further Jap raids, living on the tropical rain water which soaked them through and the few rations they had managed to save. The fortunate ones were taken off eventually by various small boats, the doubly fortunate (including Deirdre) made it to Sumatra without capture or death by disease or further bombs, and from there to Ceylon or Australia.

I dreaded telling her of Tommy's death, but it had to be done. I rehearsed it carefully to myself and stated what had happened as dispassionately as possible. Well, some of it. I saw no reason to add to her grief. We held hands, wept together and spoke of old times. We would meet frequently over the years, meetings which I loved and would look forward to eagerly.

'You know,' she said to me on one such occasion, smiling, 'I very nearly married you, not Tommy.'

'I know,' I said. We both laughed.

'He was a dear, dear man,' she said. 'A wonderful father.'

'He adored you,' I said.

'Yes . . . Do you know a funny thing? The sex thing was never great between us, I don't know why. We rarely seemed to – what shall I say? – get it right.'

Who would have thought?

'It didn't matter all that much,' she said. 'Oh, I know, in the novels and the films it's a huge thing, everything really. But in real life, our lives anyway, it was a shadow, but not a huge one . . . We always loved each other.'

Later Deirdre went to live in England. She never remarried, but lived her life happily as far as I could see. She had good children and an unflinching religious faith, not a bad recipe for a contented life. She died last year in a retirement home, mourned by her sons and her grandchildren and, most of all, by me. I loved that woman and I miss her, probably more than any of those who have gone. If there is an afterlife – could there be? Sometimes I long for it, though I cannot believe it – its greatest joy for me would be to see her again, to hear her laughter and to bask in the warmth of her presence.

Eileen, too, I finally met again, in a Dublin restaurant. Here was a surprise. At first I didn't recognize the woman who came across the crowded room towards me. She wore an obviously expensive suit and hat, with a fox fur around her shoulders. She was older, of course, but what was new to me was her self-assurance, the aura of someone who was used to being in charge of things.

She had made a success of her life, running her father's business firmly and astutely. As the small town where she lived had become more prosperous, so had she. She had earned a lot of money and invested it well. She drove an expensive car, had built herself a fine new house and had servants. She was nobody's fool. She gave orders and expected them to be obeyed. Could this be the same shy, frightened girl with whom I had once shared my life?

She kissed me firmly on the cheek. 'How are you, Tim?' she said as if we had last met a week before. The shrewd eyes looked me over. 'You're thin,' she said, 'but that's only to be expected. You must mind yourself.'

And so we talked, I and this stranger who was my wife, for, absurdly, in divorceless Ireland we were still wed in the eyes of both Church and state, after all those years of separation. We talked about our son, about Malaya and Tommy's death and Deirdre and our wider families. We talked with an intimacy – no, not intimacy, with an ease – which we had never really known when we were young. We did not talk, and never really have, about the failure of our marriage. Then we went our separate ways.

I saw her thereafter maybe every couple of years. Our relationship was courteous, easy, no more. She was a different person to the one I had married, probably I was different myself. The old ghosts had been laid, the old resentments were dead. They had become pointless.

Once, and once only, she said to me what she used to say so often – in the old days: 'We should never have married, you know,' the old refrain that used to cause me so much pain. But this time I could only agree. Who is to say by what mixture of chance and free choice most of us end up with our partners for life? Sometimes it seems to me to be no more than sheer luck, good or bad.

She died, too, some years ago, suddenly like her father before her. I attended the funeral, a huge affair, for she was well known and regarded throughout the county, but I felt a complete stranger there, hardly knowing a soul. Who would have thought that of the four of us, Eileen, Tommy, Deirdre and myself, I would be the last survivor? Grief? Yes, who could not feel some grief? Who could not remember that young girl, smiling up at me, dressed in white on that distant lawn, while a band played selections from Gilbert and Sullivan? Who could not feel for what might have been?

At the funeral I met a man of about my own age. A strong farmer, a widower, well dressed, educated, sure of himself. He came over to me afterwards and shook my hand.

'I was a friend of Eileen's for many years,' he told me. 'I'll miss her greatly.'

I knew of course. From his interest, from the way he had been staring at me. For an instant I felt a prick of the old jealousy, but straightaway I realized how absurd it was. And, after all, why not? Who was I to feel disapproval? It was too late for that years before.

What had she done that I had not done myself? I looked at him more closely. He had that slightly withdrawn look of sorrow controlled.

'I'm sorry,' I said. There was a pause between us. 'Yes,' he said, and turned away.

What went on between them? Was it a full-blown affair or, more likely, one of those arrangements you come across between middle-aged couples, friendship, companionship but nothing more? Whichever it was I know it would have been discreetly done.

I contemplated asking one of the cousins or neighbours whom I met at the funeral about it, knowing full well that, no matter how guarded they might have been, their friendship would have been the subject of wagging tongues. But it would have seemed so prying, so crass in the face of death, that I let it pass.

But all that was still in the future. At the end of that year's leave spent in Ireland after my release from the prison camp, I went back to Malaya for a last term of service before retirement. Everything was anti-climax there for me. The country was as beautiful and compelling as ever, but the world was different. Independence was coming and the old relationships had changed as the new ruling class prepared for it.

Our Chinese Communist allies of the war years were now our enemies. They had taken again to the jungle, from which they emerged to stage ambushes and kill planters. At first they had some successes, but bit by bit, inch by inch, they were cut off, pushed deeper and deeper into the wilderness. There, a handful of them fought on for years with a fanatical bravery, but their hour had passed, too. The new Malaya, now called Malaysia, if it can avoid tearing itself apart racially, will be a land devoted to the creation of wealth for the new men – or perhaps for the old men, who always held the purse strings in the background and probably still do.

At the end of a couple of years out there I had reached retirement age. What to do? Some few of us old hands stayed on, could not bear to leave the land where we had made our lives, even espoused the religion of Mohammad.

Maybe that's what I should have done, but for better or worse I wanted back to Ireland. The Malayan chapter was over for me, it was an orange that was sucked dry. I felt more of an alien there than when I had first arrived forty years earlier.

Once more I prepared to leave. Kassim had reappeared when I had returned, older like myself but still as cheerful as ever. Once more we embraced, once more said farewell, but this time there would be no return. We would not see each other again. He was a grandfather now. He had done his work and, in the proper order of things, he would return to his *kampung*, where he had been born, to live out the remainder of his span surrounded by his family. That is the way, surely, that it should be.

There was no journey by ship now, no jaunt across half the world with its exotic stops. Crammed like sardines into a box we were hurled across a dozen countries in a plane, and were back in Europe bleary-eyed within a day. *Sic transit*, eh?

I bought this house here, because it was in a place where there were other retired ex-colonials. I see them occasionally, shuffling around, old like myself and complaining about the cold. What was it they used to say in the country? A fire is half of life to the old people. For us who spent so much time in the sun, the raw damp chill of these watery islands pervades our very bones, so that we spend half our remaining lives huddling over the flames. But even worse is the darkness that closes in for so much of the year and we dream literally, as in the song, of the light of other days.

The years pass quickly by, despite the loneliness and the sameness of my days. In my dreams they come and go – Tommy, Eileen, Deirdre, Malays and Chinese and Japs, Campbell the planter who killed himself, Kassim who was my friend and my driver.

In my sleep last night I found myself in a strange bedroom. On the bed lay a baby girl, some five or six months of age. She was incredibly beautiful, a small rose, glowing in skin, glowing in hair, glowing in clear blue eyes. I bent down to lift her up, but she turned into an old, old woman in a white bed gown. She looked at me, at first uncomprehending. Then she stretched her arms out to me. 'Robert,' she said, lovingly. I know no Robert. She stretched out her arms to draw me into her embrace, and as she did so she died. I was frightened. I pulled back and turned to leave the room. In the doorway stood another girl, this one six or seven years old. She wore a white dress with a bow, and her hair was done in ringlets. She was dressed as girls used to dress in the early part of the century. I awoke, frightened. What did it mean?

I am looking at myself in the mirror. I will say:

'Of all the fruits of the Malay peninsula the most fascinating is the durian. How can one describe its flavour, or perhaps I should say flavours? Imagine the finest strawberries, raspberries, plums and pineapples, all set in the lightest and most delicious of custards . . .'

I open my mouth. All that comes out is 'Wah, wah, wah . . .'

The heavens will crack. Even the jungle will not survive. The great trees, the twisted vines, the bushes, the animals will burn and wither and turn to ashes. Their atoms will split and be sucked into nothingness. But the universe will spin on its great circle, light will drift across the aeons, and the great engine of life, unimaginable, will turn and turn and turn . . .

I hear a car stopping outside the door. There are foot-steps on the gravel.

Elaine Feinstein
Lady Chatterley's Confession 10 Guineas

From one of our most distinguished authors and a recognized expert on Lawrence comes an extraordinary sequel to a legendary and bestselling novel.

In the voice of Lady Chatterley, Elaine Feinstein picks up the lives of two of the literary world's most famous lovers and carries on their poignant story.

Caught up in their passion for one another, Connie and Mellors try to escape scandal and prejudice by running away to Tuscany with their young daughter Emily. But will Italian society perceive them as equals? Will Connie be able to pass as the wife of a servant, or Mellors tolerate her acceptance as the wayward aristocrat? And can their love survive the indignity of an everyday relationship?

From the class-ridden depression of England before the war, to Italy as Fascism begins to clamp down, Connie is forced into decisions guided only by her heart. The future holds uncertainty however she looks at it, but ultimately, with her daughter as evidence of a great love, she has the hope and courage that Mellors has given her, and the knowledge that simply to be alive is a privilege.

'A lovely book. A novel about what women do, not what they're meant to do'

Fay Weldon

Larry Watson
Montana 1948 £9.99

'From the summer of my twelfth year I carry a series of images more vivid and lasting than any others of my boyhood and indelible beyond all attempts the years make to erase or fade them . . .'

Montana 1948; and the events of one cataclysmic summer will for ever alter twelve-year-old David Hayden's view of his family. His father, a small-town sheriff; his remarkably strong-willed mother; his uncle, a war hero and respected doctor; and the family's Sioux housekeeper, Marie Little Soldier, whose shocking revelations form the heart of the story.

   As their memories unravel before young David's eyes, he comes to learn that the truth is not what you believe it to be. That power is abused. And that sometimes you have to choose between loyalty and justice . . .

Brilliantly evoking both time and place, Larry Watson recounts David's age-old tale of childhood lost and adulthood gained. *Montana 1948* is a new classic to stand alongside *To Kill a Mocking Bird* and *The Go-Between*.

'A wonderful book'
                    Louise Erdrich

'As universal in its themes as it is original in its particularities, *Montana 1948* is a significant addition to the fiction of the American West'
                    Washington Post

Cindy Bonner
Lily £9.99

'Folks round here say the Beatty boys were just plain wild and no good, and that they made us all look bad in the eyes of the rest of Texas. Like we were all wild and no good ourselves, to have grown up such bad boys, like that Beatty bunch.'

Young Lily DeLony tells her version of what happened on Christmas Eve 1883 in the town of McDade, Texas, when a vigilante group of ordinary citizens struck against a gang of outlaws. One of the outlaw gang was to become the love of Lily's life. One of vigilantes was her father.

This father's word is law and is seldom spoken softly. Lily is a strong, upright girl who knows the rules of virtue and righteousness, and follows them. Follows them, that is, until she meets Marion 'Shot' Beatty, youngest of the Beatty brothers, when this good girl falls so in love with a bad boy that she forsakes everything to ride with him – outlaw and fugitive that he is.

The spirit and fearlessness of Lily's character shine through this utterly convincing, beguiling and moving first novel.

'Vivid and romantic. Like her heroine, Lily, author Cindy Bonner shows a great heart'

Deirdre Purcell

Elizabeth Buchan
Perfect Love £14.99

Are we tough enough and bold enough to survive the modern marriage?

Prue and Max Valour thought so. There are twenty years' difference in their ages but they have enjoyed two decades of marriage – from the moment when a nineteen-year-old Prue listened to the account of Max's disastrous first marriage to Helen and decided to cherish Max with all the fervour and burning conviction of a modern Joan of Arc.

What Prue had forgotten was Violet, Max and Helen's rebellious and terrified seven-year-old who grieved for her mother, and could not forgive Prue for being the woman her father chose to love instead. Now, with a successful career forged in New York, a husband, Jamie, and a baby, Violet is back and, once again, Prue must cope with her stepdaughter.

But life has a way of throwing in the unexpected and contented, busy Prue finds herself precipitated into a passionate love affair that shakes her to the core and marks the beginining of a secret life. And what of Max who spends his spare time fishing and polishing his guns? Experience certainly brings a toughness and realism, but is theory quite the same thing as practice?

The small village of Dainton and the city are very different places and as Prue moves between these two worlds, between innocence and new-found knowledge, between the gluttony and surrender of desire and the stark realities that ensue, the author pinpoints the extraordinary bargains and accommodations struck between people who love one another.

'What a good writer Buchan is' *Daily Telegraph*

'Is Buchan the new Trollope? . . . a terrific new novel . . . Buchan's compassionate novel has an integral wisdom' *Daily Mail*

**From the prize-winning author of *Consider the Lily*
'The literary equivalent of an English country garden'
*Sunday Times***

Jay Rayner
The Marble Kiss £5.99

1483. In a Tuscan castle Princess Joanna dei Strosetti dies in the agony of childbirth. Her son will ensure the immortality of the family, her husband will enshrine her beauty in a tomb.

Five hundred years later the tomb is restored, but for art historian Robert Kelner the work has desecrated his greatest passion. His disagreement with the restorer takes him to a Florentine courtroom, but the two men share one thing: their love for Joanna, a woman who has been dead half a mellenium.

Journalist Alex Fuller, wearily covering what he sees as another tedious art-world squabble, is unimpressed by his expenses-paid trip to Florence – until he meets Isabella dei Strosetti, Joanna's beautiful descendant.

Little by little, Alex is drawn into the cold heart of an old, old mystery – only to find that the ashes of love are smouldering still . . .

'History, art and the rites of passion are wound intriguingly into a dazzling debut'
Cosmopolitan

'A terrific page-turner and a real joy to read . . . a brilliant debut'
Literary Review